I0593837

LILAC IN WINTER

LILAC IN WINTER

A NOVEL

Susan Pogorzelski

BROWN BEAGLE BOOKS

Pennsylvania

Copyright © 2019 by Susan Pogorzelski

This book is a work of fiction. Names, characters, locales, and incidents are products of the author's imagination or are used fictitiously.

All rights reserved. No portion of this book may be reproduced, distributed, or transmitted in any form or by any means, or stored in a database, storage, or retrieval system, without the prior written permission of the publisher.

This novel contains an excerpt from the poem, "Stopping by Woods on a Snowy Evening" by Robert Frost (1922). This poem entered the public domain on January 1, 2019.

Brown Beagle Books, Lititz, PA
www.brownbeaglebooks.com

ISBN Paperback: 978-0-9888751-7-3
ISBN Digital: 978-0-9888751-8-0
LCCN: 2019900491

Cover Design by Andrew Brown, designforwriters.com
Interior Design by Rebecca Brown, designforwriters.com

Visit the author's website at www.susanpogorzelski.com

Printed in the United States of America

For Joshua

The woods are lovely, dark and deep,
But I have promises to keep,
And miles to go before I sleep,
And miles to go before I sleep.

– from "Stopping by Woods on a Snowy Evening"
by Robert Frost

Chapter One

LILAC

16 YEARS, 11 MONTHS, 3 WEEKS, 0 DAYS

My name is Lilac Sophia Carpenter, and I'm sixteen years old.

I'm going to be sixteen years old for the rest of my life.

SPRING

Chapter Two

LILAC

I'm fourteen today. Yesterday I was forty-three. Maybe tomorrow I'll want to be nine. I never know what the wish might be from one day to the next.

But I decide I'm fourteen today because it sounds like a good age, a reasonable age. At least when you're taken to the hospital for the first time when you're fourteen, you're young enough to believe they can actually save you and innocent enough to think you have a whole lifetime left.

And besides. Imagining I'm fourteen today isn't so far off from the truth.

When I wake up this time, there's someone new in the room. I can sense him there before I open my eyes, hear the subtle crack of his joints when he shifts his weight, the scratch of his pen when he scrawls his name. I imagine him standing in the doorway in a long white lab coat and pale blue scrubs, sneakers on his feet. Maybe he's young and in his first-year residency. Maybe he's old and calculating the days until retirement. Maybe he's somewhere in between.

I can picture where he's standing. After two years and dozens of visits, I know every square-inch of this room by now. I know the tan speckled tile that lays beneath my bed, know the faded yellow walls that hold up a dry-erase board with my name and date of birth and a nurse's unfortunate drawing of Winnie-the-Pooh. I know the scrape of dried leaves collecting in the hollow outside my window, the rattle of the dinner cart and the one wheel that always seems to stick. I know this symphony of sound: intercoms and whispers and prayers. I know how to listen. I've learned how to forget.

I know everyone who walks in and out of here.

I don't know him.

It's daylight out, the middle of spring. I know the curtains are pulled open because I can feel the warmth of the sunlight on my face. In a few hours, when the sun rises higher and the fever sets in, they'll draw the shades and place damp washcloths on my forehead to help keep me cool, but now it's pleasant, like the stray heat from a recently turned-off stove.

I blink a few times to scatter the lingering dreams and focus on him. He's where I thought he would be—standing in the open doorway, flipping through the pages of my chart. But instead of a lab coat and scrubs, he's wearing black pants and a light blue dress shirt, the sleeves rolled up casually to the elbows. There's a pair of thick-framed glasses in one hand, and he frowns and squints at the pages before exhaling a small sigh.

I know the words he's read.

I stretch my legs and readjust my head against the pillows, finding a cool place to rest my cheek. He looks up, and when he sees I'm awake, he tucks the chart beneath his arm and puts on his glasses and smiles. I decide I like his smile. It reaches his dark eyes, makes them light up, and that light is contagious. I want to smile back, but it's too soon.

I may know him now, but he still doesn't know me.

"Didn't wake you, did I?" His voice is rich and deep in a way that seems to match his age. He crosses the few steps towards my bed, lays the chart on the blankets by my feet, and checks the IV bag hanging above me.

I point to the empty chocolate pudding cup on the bedside table. "Would you give me more of the good stuff if I say yes?"

His smile widens. "They said you had a sense of humor."

"Yeah, well…" I force myself to sit up and glance at the empty chair beside my bed. "Where's my mom?"

"Out in the hallway on a phone call. I'm sure she'll be right in."

"And my dad?"

"Afraid I haven't seen him."

No, of course not. That was two years ago when he was still trying to be a father, not today. He wouldn't be here today, not if he can help it.

"My name's Dr. Wilhems," the man introduces himself. "I'm the consulting physician here. I'll be checking in on you every once in a while, if that's okay with you." He picks up the chart again and flips through the pages. "Can you give me your name and date of birth, sweetheart?"

Outside, a cloud eclipses the sun, casting shadows across the room. I frown and glance at the dry-erase board where my birthdate is written in black marker next to a too-thin, honey-loving bear.

I don't like the way he calls me sweetheart. There's something minimizing, juvenile about it. Then I remember I'm fourteen today—that the date on the dry-erase board is wrong—and I shake my head.

"Come back later," I say. "Maybe tomorrow. I'll know for sure then."

Chapter Three

If I had to look back and pick a point where my life really began, I'd say it was the day I met Nathan Emery. It's like the years before him don't exist anymore because now I can't imagine my life without him. From the time we were kids and he moved in next door, we've met at every crossroad, converged at every fork in the road, circled our way around and joined at every juncture.

Life always seems to lead back to him.

We're six years old and making castles out of mud by the creek that runs through our backyards. It's late July—that time of year when the grass begins to brown and the pavement cracks and the sunlight casts a nostalgic glow across the landscape. Soon we'll be going school shopping for new backpacks and pencil cases, if we're lucky and they're on sale, but today we've dragged the garden hose all the way across the yard to fill in the creek that's been dried out by the drought, wriggling our hands and bare feet into the creek bed as we imagine we're sifting through sand on the beach.

"You can't put that there," Nathan says.

I stare at the pile of mud I've just slopped on top of a bare stretch of grass. "Why not?"

"Cause that's where the ramparts go."

I don't tell him I don't know what a rampart is or where it is or isn't supposed to go. He speaks with such conviction that I automatically believe him, and I know from that moment on, I'll never doubt a word he says. All because he knows what a rampart is at six years old.

"Well, what about here?" I move the glop of mud a little further left. His dog—a golden retriever named Lucky— sits up and sniffs at the mud, then rolls back on his side with a groan.

Nathan hesitates and scrunches up his face, then shrugs. "Yeah, okay," he says and turns back to his tower.

In exactly one hour, a moving truck will pull up in front of the house next door, and a man with a booming voice and heavy accent will barrel out of the garage, gesturing wildly at his bare wrist and the few boxes that litter the drive- way next to the family van. The commotion will cause my mother to glance out the kitchen window, where she's been preparing a barely-edible ham and broccoli casserole for our new neighbors—a middle-aged couple from New Jersey with two teenage girls and one six-year-old boy named Nathan. She'll notice the hose draped across the patio furniture and will follow it along, snaking its way through the grass, until she spies us under a pair of willow trees, digging a moat around our fortress with two teaspoons I snuck from the dishwasher when she wasn't looking. Her eyes will grow wide at the sight of us—mud reaching past our elbows and caking our shorts—and she'll slam open the back door and race across the yard, shouting for us to back away from the mud and, no, don't we dare come near her. Her shouts will catch the attention of Nathan's father, who'll holler into the house until his mother marches across the yard, pauses to exchange a few pleasantries with my mother, then grabs him by a dry corner of his shirt sleeve and ushers him back home, an unhappy dog at their heels.

In the bath, I'll pull clumps of mud from my long hair and watch with delight as they get caught in the drain. At bedtime, I'll change into a fresh nightgown and whisper my daily prayer for a dog like his, and before I slide beneath the cool sheets, I'll sneak a look out the window at our castle.

Six weeks later, on a wind-swept September morning, I'll greet him at the end of our driveway. I'll be wearing a brand-new Cinderella backpack. He'll be carrying a Superman lunchbox. We'll climb the steps of the bus and slide into the seat next to each other while our mothers stand side-by-side, their second mug of coffee in hand, and wave us off, but we won't pay them any attention. He's already busy explaining what a turret is.

That's how I like to imagine our story beginning.

It isn't anywhere close to the truth.

Chapter Four

NATHAN

My story doesn't begin here. But if my sister has her way, it'll end here—

"I swear to God, Nathan. If I find one more cereal bowl in your room…"

—right here in the middle of her kitchen, bludgeoned to death by dishware.

They're empty threats that lead nowhere, that's what they are, and she knows it. Her husband, Tim, knows it. Even my baby nephew knows it, judging by the spit-filled grin he has on his face. I cross my eyes and stick my tongue out at him before diving back into my Cap'n Crunch, milk spilling over the tip of the spoon and back into the Tupperware container.

My sister lowers her arms over the sink, successfully transplanting the half a dozen ceramic bowls where she thinks they rightfully belong.

"I was gonna do it after school," I mumble, taking another bite, refusing to turn around and meet her death glare.

But she isn't even listening. She's on a full-blown tirade, a symphony of clanging bowls and tinging silverware marked by a crescendo of words as she loads the dishwasher, pointing out what we can all do to help out around here, now that she has another person to cook for, because it's not enough that she has a husband and a toddler and a full-time job—oh, no. Now she has a little brother to look after, too, and it's not like she hasn't been doing that for most of her life, anyway.

I freeze.

She gasps.

Even my nephew stops slamming his spoon on his tray and stares at her.

"Nate…"

"It's cool, Jess."

"Nathan…"

"It's fine, just forget it."

Across the table, Tim glances between the two of us before standing and taking his proper cereal bowl to the sink. In the window's reflection, I can see him kiss her temple, see the sag of her shoulders as she leans into him.

She didn't mean it. I know she didn't. My sister's the kind of person who says shit without thinking. Still, the words stab at something inside of me, twist around in my gut for a while, and I shovel another spoonful of cereal into my mouth and try not to let it get to me.

"I'll get Jasper cleaned up for daycare," Tim says. A second later, he's lifting a giggling one-year-old out of his high-chair. "Come on, buddy. Let's get rid of that stinky you've got going on."

Jess slides into Tim's empty seat across from me. I can feel her stare even without looking at her, can feel the waiting, the something-coming.

She wants to talk.

I let go of my spoon, watch it dip against the side of the bowl before disappearing into the remaining milk. That's always the best part—the leftover milk. Let the cereal get soggy enough and some of the sugar residue will dissolve, creating a kind of warm milkshake. It really is the best part.

But not today.

"Sorry about the dishes," I begin at the same time she says, "I shouldn't have said that."

She opens her mouth to speak again, closes it, then takes a deep breath. "It's an adjustment, you know? There's so much going on with work and then coming home to Jasper and Tim, and it's just been a rough few months. But I'm glad you're here."

"I can always stay with Jamie."

"Jamie..." Her voice trails off, and she waves her hand dismissively. "She has her own stuff going on. And besides," she smiles, and I realize how much she looks like Mom when she does, "I like having my baby brother around. Helps with the babysitting."

I snort. "Yeah. Right."

She taps her nails on the table, picks an apple out of the fruit bowl in the center, studies it for bruising, then places it back just as quickly.

"You want to ask if I'm ever going back." My sister may be ten years older than me, but I can still read her like a book.

"Are you?"

I scoot back in my chair, scratching the legs against the linoleum, and grab the Tupperware bowl. "No."

"Nathan—"

"I can't live there, Jess. I—"

I'm cut short by Jasper running back into the kitchen, heading straight for Jess's lap.

Just as well. I don't want to talk about this, anyway.

She lifts him high into the air— "There's my baby boy!"—and grabs the cereal box in her other hand, kissing Tim on the cheek as she passes him in the doorway. The choreography is flawless.

The married life suits my oldest sister, but even though she has the cool husband and the cutest kid ever and the old rowhome across the river on the other side of town from where we grew up, sometimes I'll catch her looking around her house—at everything she's created for herself—with a wistful smile on her face. As soon as she sees me watching her, she'll shake it away with a roll of her eyes and a comment about how the house still needs so much work done to it, like she wants to pretend family life and home renovations isn't everything she's always wanted.

I don't know, maybe it's easier for her that way. Maybe it lets her cope with the guilt of leaving home at eighteen and never looking back. Maybe that's why she's always getting on me about having done the same—not for the fact that I'm encroaching on her dream life, but because I'm not willing to wait in hell for another year.

"I'll see you guys later." I tousle Jasper's hair and head for the front door, grabbing my backpack from a bench in the hallway and slinging it over my shoulder.

"Wait, you don't have your truck," Jess hollers after me.

"I'm picking it up after school."

"So, I'll drive you."

"I'm taking the bus."

"I'll drive you," she says again.

"But—"

Behind my sister, Tim is shaking his head, and I sigh and drop my bag. "Sure, Jess. You can drive me."

She grins and stretches her arms out for her son, who gleefully waddles into them again. "Good. Now come here, my little man!"

I step outside to wait on the porch just as the school bus ambles by. So much for that option.

"You have everything?" she asks, pulling the door shut behind her.

I pat my bag in response and follow her down the walk to the sedan that's parked along the curb, folding myself into the passenger seat, backpack on the floorboard between my legs.

We drive in silence for a while, a morning radio show on low, though neither of us are listening. I stare out the window and watch the flow of the river until we round a corner and the water is replaced by a blur of buildings that make up Hastings Corporate Center.

"So…"

I groan and lean my head back. "Can we please not talk about it?"

She purses her lips and taps her fingers against the steering wheel. I think all is safe until she takes another breath. "How's Lila?"

The question is so out of left field, I turn to stare at her for a few seconds, not sure I heard her correctly.

"Lila…" Jess says again, more slowly this time. She raises an eyebrow at me like I'm an idiot before turning her attention back to the road. "How's she doing?"

I shrug my shoulders and stare straight ahead.

"I thought you were close with her?"

"I was." I don't want to talk about this, either. I don't want to talk about anything. It's all in the past, anyway—doesn't she get that? "I guess she's fine," I mutter.

"Mom says she's back in the hospital."

My head shoots up at this, trying to figure out if she's kidding or not. But no, why would my sister be kidding about this? "Since when?"

"Since I talked to Mom yesterday." Jess curses at a teenage driver, who flips her off, then makes a hard left into the school parking lot. "Are you going to see her?"

The words spin around in my head. I haven't had a full conversation with Lilac in months—since after her sister's wedding, and even that was the first time we'd spoken in years. And when was the last time I saw her in school? We were supposed to have Astronomy together this semester. I saw her name on the class roster, but I assumed she dropped it when she never showed up for class—I thought maybe it was me she was trying to avoid, the way we've avoided each other all these years. Occasionally, we'd pass each other in the hall, our eyes locking, but we'd never say so much as hello. Once in a while, we'd sit near each other in the library, but our history was a barricade between us beckoning more silence.

I shake my head. "I don't think she wants to see me."

She definitely doesn't want to see me. Not after that night. Not after what I did.

Jess puts the car into park and frowns. "I mean Mom," she says. "She misses you, you know."

I sigh and gather my backpack, mad at myself for somehow getting roped back into this discussion. "Well, I guess she would."

"You have to sort this out, Nathan," Jess calls after me as I step out of the car.

I sling my backpack over my shoulder and walk away.

Not today, I don't.

Chapter Five

I'm sixty-six today. It seems like a good age, a sturdy age. Retirement age. When I look in the mirror, the girl I was stares back through familiar eyes, though she wears locks of graying hair and a lifetime of laugh lines. My hands have become wrinkled and arthritic after all these years of working—signing documents as an assistant at a Fortune 500, perhaps, or ringing up customers at a small, independent bake shop at the mall. They're hands that have held lovers and fed children, hands that have raised in protest and joined together in prayer.

Today, there's fresh soil beneath my fingernails, dirt in the creases of my palms. I've spent the morning working in the garden, pausing only to come inside and make myself a pitcher of iced tea.

It's early in May, but we're already experiencing a heatwave, and I take off my gardening hat and shake the sweat free from my hair. My husband is sitting in the recliner in the living room, finishing his coffee and newspaper as he's done every Sunday morning for the past forty-three years. From front to back and all the inserts, he'll pore over every article, every caption, every obituary. Then at lunchtime, he'll relay the most interesting pieces of news. Today, it'll be the fact that Michael Kelly from our daughter's church is marrying for the third time, followed by a quip about how lucky we were to get it right on one.

We've fallen into a nice rhythm in life. Lovers to best friends to partners—or maybe it's the reverse. We marry at age twenty-three and have our first child—a daughter—a year later. It's the three of us for two years, living in a cramped apartment with a view of the river and an oven that's always on the fritz. We wouldn't have it any other way. It's the challenges that define us, we say to each other, and then we make love on the kitchen table or the sofa and twice in the bed.

There are times now when we remember the love of our youth. When we go for long summer drives down winding country roads, he pulls to a stop beside a roadside stand to buy a fresh-cut bouquet of wildflowers that reminds us of our wedding day. When we picnic in the park, listening to shouts from children on the playground, we smile and recall pushing each other on the swings.

Twice a year, for our birthdays, we'll go out to dinner at a little Italian bistro on the corner of Main and Spruce Street. I'll wear my best silk dress and those high heels that kill my feet, and he'll wear a suit and the tie I got him for Christmas. His eyes will light up when he sees me at the top of the stairs, and he'll shake his head and say, "I was one lucky bastard the day I met you."

My cheeks will flush like I'm a teenager again, and he'll place a kiss on my cheek, smelling like spearmint toothpaste. He stopped wearing aftershave years ago. Then he'll walk me out to the car, and we'll sneak glances at each other on the drive to the restaurant where we'll eat lobster ravioli at a corner table set for two. That night, like every night, we'll remember what it's like to choose each other and fall in love all over again.

"Fridges are on sale at that appliance place near the mall," he calls from the living room.

I put a glass pitcher in the sink and run the tap. "What's wrong with our fridge?"

"It's twenty years old." He pauses. "And I thought you wanted stainless steel."

"What I want is to redo the entire kitchen." I shut the water off and transfer the pitcher to the counter, passing the tear in the wallpaper and scratched cabinet doors that still hold the scars from our second daughter's crayon exhibit.

My husband folds his newspaper and glances into the kitchen, his eyes sweeping over the outdated light fixtures and ceiling that could use a fresh coat of paint. He lifts a hand to his mouth, rubs his fingers across his chin. He's calculating the cost and amount of work in his head. We know each other too well.

"It's been twenty years," I remind him gently, stirring in the powdered tea mix.

"New cabinets?" he asks.

"We can make do with new hardware."

"And the floors?"

"I want tile, not laminate. I told you that when we moved in."

"And the stove?" His mouth twitches into a smile, and I grin back.

"As long as it works, the stove can stay."

He nods and gets up from his chair—more slowly now that his back's been giving him problems—and carries his empty mug into the kitchen. He rinses it in the sink and puts it straight into the top rack of the dishwasher, then steps behind me and wraps his arms around my waist, kisses me on the cheek. He smells like coffee. I close my eyes and lean back against him.

"It's a good stove," he whispers.

"It's an old stove," I say.

"It's a reliable stove."

I raise my eyebrows and twist around to look at him. "Reliable? That's what you come up with?"

He laughs, a low chuckle that warms me from the inside out, and nuzzles his nose into my neck. "A beautiful stove. A sexy stove."

"Nathan!"

"A hot stove."

The iced tea is forgotten on the counter.

That's how it is when I'm sixty-six.

Chapter Six

LILAC

Dr. Wilhems is wearing a lab coat the next time I see him. It contrasts against the warmth of his skin tone, makes him seem cold and more rigid, like he actually belongs here in this building filled with machines and routines. I don't like him in that lab coat. It makes me nervous, unsettled. Seeing him wear it is a stark reminder of where I am, that I belong here, too.

"I'm going over your latest lab results, Lilac," he says, flipping through my chart. I make a face when he says my name, and he notices and pauses.

"Lila," I correct him.

Sometimes I imagine my parents named me Lilac after the flower, like I was conceived in a meadow or a prairie or a private garden on some royal estate, but really, I think they were just high on paint fumes after rushing to get the nursery ready. I guess that's what happens when your baby's born three weeks early. I'd bet all my last functioning organs my mother glanced at the label on the paint can, said, "That works, now get me to the damn hospital," and then signed my birth certificate still hopped up on painkillers.

Lilac Sophia. Named after my grandmother and a can of purple paint. I mean, it could be worse. They could have gone with Petunia Pink.

I started calling myself Lila sometime around the fourth grade, after some of the kids at school decided my name was something worth making fun of despite knowing me my entire life. After a full week of only answering to Lila, the name stuck and the kids, susceptible the way kids are, I guess, moved on to teasing someone else.

All but one.

"And?" I raise my eyebrows, waiting for the news from Dr. Wilhems. I know what's coming. There's never any change.

I watch his frown deepen. "Maybe I should wait for your mother," he says.

It's because I'm eleven years old today. Adults never want to tell kids the truth if it's bad news. I've learned that a hundred times over in my life.

"Sure," I reply, only because I don't feel like hearing what he has to say. Like I said, nothing's going to change, anyway.

"Can we make you more comfortable? Anything you need?" he asks, and I think that's nice of him. The others didn't even try—they were in and out in less than five minutes. To them, I was just one more patient to be seen in the day, just another chart with all the wrong numbers.

"Got any more chocolate pudding?"

Dr. Wilhems smiles. "I'll ask the cafeteria myself."

He pats my leg and leaves the room, and I lean back against the pillows and look out the window, but the view of the river is obstructed by a financial building across the street.

It's hard being eleven. I don't know why I chose that age today. When you're eleven, all you want to do is ride bikes to the park so you can play on the merry-go-round, spinning around and around until the world becomes a blur. You want to study the globe in your classroom and hang maps on your walls at home and stick red pushpins in the countries you think you'll travel to someday. You want to spend a clear winter night charting constellations through your telescope with the boy next door, imagining what it's like to journey across galaxies when the earth feels too small.

When you're eleven, you don't want to be confined to one place. You want to run from disappointment, hide from humiliation. When you're eleven, you want to be everywhere and nowhere at once.

I don't know why I chose eleven. I won't be eleven again.

Chapter Seven

NATHAN

The stars don't really look like this.

That's all I can think as I lean my head against the edge of the wooden seat, legs spread in front of me, staring up at the scattering of light on the ceiling of the school's planetarium. These stars are false stars—only an illusion meant to teach us where to find the constellations during Earth's rotating seasons. They don't look like this.

First of all, there are billions of stars in the sky, and on a clear winter's night, you can lay on your back on a sleeping bag, bundled in five layers of clothing, and begin to believe you can actually count them all. That's how bright they are. That's how close they feel. That's how they seem to see straight through you, like they aren't just massive balls of burning gas millions of light years away, but living energy whispering their secrets and letting you tell them yours.

But these… These stars…

Nothing but pinpricks of light.

"Who can name this constellation?"

"Her name's Janet."

Dan Henry. Kind of a prick himself.

An elbow nudges my side, and I roll my eyes and try to ignore him.

This class is an easy "A." I've been studying the stars with Lilac since we were ten years old. I should be in the advanced class—learning about dark matter and superclusters and Kepler's laws—not this introductory class where the constellations are outlined for us so we can better decipher them. But this was a pre-requisite, and I needed to fill an elective. Tried telling all of this to Mr. Vick, but he wouldn't hear of it. Now he's regretting it. Or at least he was, when I began answering every question while barely paying attention.

That was at the beginning of the semester. Now I don't say much in class. The second week in, I fastened myself at the back of the room, and now I'll listen with half an ear for anything interesting while I doodle cartoons in my notebook. It gives me something to do. Every once in a while, I'll catch Mr. Vick glancing at me. I can't tell if he'd rather have me talking nonstop or staying silent. I'd rather stay silent like this. It lets me think. With the false stars above me, I can imagine I'm ten years old again—before everything went to hell with Lilac the first time. I can pretend I'm on my back beside her in the space between our houses, charting the planets and taking turns looking through her brand-new telescope, poking at each other when we see finally see what we think is Mars but I discovered in class yesterday was really Jupiter.

I should tell Lilac.

The thought startles me so much, I sit up, which causes Mr. Vick to stop speaking for a minute and stare at me as if I'm actually from outer space.

I want to tell Lilac.

I wish I could.

I wish I could run across the yards and right through her front door, say hi to her mom and take the stairs two at a time until I reach her room. I wish I could see her there, sprawled on the bed with her nose in a book, and tell her that it's Jupiter, not Mars, and that we've been wrong all this time.

I should be there. She should be here, in class.

But she's not.

Besides, the planets don't matter anymore. There's too much left unspoken between us, too much else to talk about. Too much we might never get the chance to say.

We're light years apart now and growing farther and farther away each day.

Chapter Eight

Sometimes I wonder what life would have been like if Nathan hadn't moved in next door when he was six. What if his parents didn't like the portico or the gables or the narrow front porch and chose the modern house with the view of the river instead? What if we didn't ride the bus to school every day or dig for dinosaur bones in the creek out back every afternoon? What if we didn't run across the yards to attend each other's birthday parties, what if we didn't ever look at the stars?

What if, for all these years, we were only strangers?

OK. I guess we'll go there and see how this one turns out...

We know each other on the periphery the way most people know their mailman or their hairstylist or that one bagger at the grocery store. A face. Maybe a name. But rarely anything more. Every so often, we'll glance at each other as we pass in the hallways at school. Once in a while, our eyes will meet across the crowded cafeteria tables at lunch. But it's nothing more than fleeting curiosity. Just a flicker of recognition, a mild interest, an acknowledgement that here's someone in the world who doesn't mean anything to us yet, but maybe for one moment, someday, they will.

We have first-period art together our freshman year of high school. We've never had a class together before, and I wonder how that can be, after all these years in the same district. We take our seats, his eyes skimming the room for someone familiar until they land on me. I see the slight arch of his eyebrows, the question casting a shadow in his eyes.

Do I know you?

Nope. I'm just another face in the crowd. Just another voice piping up from the back of the room. He's nobody to me. I'm nothing to him.

Mr. Berber claps his hands, and we all quiet down and turn around to face the front of the room, waiting for him to take attendance.

"Everyone here?" he asks. "Good. Let's get started."

Mr. Berber will go down in our personal history as the coolest teacher we'll ever have. The first week of school, he wears old concert t-shirts featuring Led Zeppelin and The Doors, which wins approval from at least half the kids in the class and nonchalance from the others. But then he gets reamed out by the principal and begins wearing button-down dress shirts, his long hair pulled back in a ponytail and his gray goatee trimmed so he looks like every other teacher and their dad.

He holds up a finger when he walks in the door wearing a tweed blazer and carrying a brown leather briefcase. Then he dumps the blazer and briefcase on the floor in a corner and rolls up the sleeves of his shirt, and we spy the familiar tie-dye of a Grateful Dead t-shirt through the thin fabric. He notices us whispering to each other because he winks, closes the door, and pops in a CD. A second later, an electric guitar pierces the air.

"Let this be a lesson for all of you," he says. "They can dress you up, but they can't take away who you are. Or what you are." Then he grabs a paintbrush, tosses it in the air the way I've seen drummers do on TV, and yells, "Let's get to work!"

We spend the first semester learning the basics. Perspective. Shading. Texture. We sketch trees and fruit and scenery. We create self-portraits out of newspaper and magazines. We make clay molds from old shoes and render our personalities on them. I paint purple polka dots. At the table across the aisle from me, I notice Nathan coating his shoe with a simple layer of dark blue.

"An ocean?"

He looks up at me, like he's startled I've said anything, and I realize I've spoken out loud and now *I'm* startled I've said anything. But there they are. The words are between us. We're not just aware of each other's existence anymore, we're in each other's lives, if only for this brief second, and there's no going back.

He shakes his head and glances down, runs the tip of his brush against the sole of the shoe. He doesn't say anything.

"Sky?" I guess again because it's too late now. I'm already way too deep in this.

"No," he says, and I frown.

"Blueberries?" The girl on the other side of him glares at me, but I can't stop myself. "Rainclouds? Robin's eggs? Oh! The moon?"

"It's nothing, okay?" There's an anger in his voice I don't expect, and I clamp my mouth shut. He must see the surprise in my eyes because he sighs and ducks his head, his eyes focused back on his artwork. When he speaks again, his voice is quieter, remorse buried somewhere nearby. "It represents nothing."

I don't get it. I don't know what I said that was so bad, but when I try to make conversation with him again at the sink, he scrubs at his brushes wordlessly, then walks away as soon as he can.

We don't talk again for weeks.

When we walk into class the Monday after winter break, the chalkboard is covered with images of significant moments in history. Soldiers raising a flag atop a pile of rubble. Astronauts walking on the moon. A newspaper cutout proclaiming the fall of the Berlin Wall. On the floor below the chalkboard is a plastic toy chest filled with odd materials: twigs and yarn and metal coils. A collection of Legos. Modeling clay. Old machine parts and screws and magnets affixed to sheet metal.

"What's up with all this, Mr. B?" CJ Bartlett calls out from the back of the room.

"This," Mr. Berber announces, "is your next project. The convergence of two of the most powerful abstract ideas: history and art." He holds up a hand. "'Ah, but Mr. B,' I can hear you saying. 'History isn't abstract.'" We pause and glance at each other. We're pretty sure no one is saying that, but Mr. Berber continues anyway. "But isn't it? Isn't it? Isn't history just the retelling of a story? And what is art if not the visual expression of that story?

"So, my young savants," he says, crossing to the front of the room and pointing to the chalkboard. "You'll each be assigned a significant event in history and use art to tell its story. And because in this room I get to play God, I'll choose your event and your partner for you." He scans the room, then points to me and Nathan. "You two. Pair up."

"What?"

"Come on…"

Yep. This isn't going to go well. We spend the rest of the class period barely talking as we try to plan our project around D-Day, but it feels like World War II between us. Only a little less…explosive. Nathan refuses to look at me when I ask him if he wants to make a replica of Normandy out of Legos, so I, in turn, decide to ignore him.

The next day, I make it even easier on him. I don't show up to school at all.

I'm stuck in the hospital for three days while they run a battery of tests on me because they can't figure out how to get my fever down or why my muscles have suddenly decided not to work. When I'm finally home, it's nearly February and another full week before I'm feeling well enough to go back to school.

That's the way it really happened. But we're not talking about what really happened. Not now, anyway…

Mr. Berber claps his hands together when he sees me sitting across the aisle from Nathan. "You're both back. Good. Your project's due today."

I whirl around to look at Nathan. He looks just as surprised as I do.

Mr. Berber raises his eyebrows. "No project? Interesting, interesting… You can both come in at lunch to work. Moving on!"

I'm the first to arrive to the empty classroom at lunchtime, so I head to the back where the toy chest now sits and kneel beside it, digging for stray Lego pieces. I don't hear him come up behind me, but he drops his backpack and kneels down beside me. I pause and glance at him, then add a plastic palm tree to the pile of colorful bricks between us.

"Why didn't you do the project?" he asks me.

"Why didn't you?"

"I wasn't here."

"Well, neither was I."

We stare at each other, at a stalemate. No one will be the winner today—not when our grade is on the line and we're both at risk of losing.

He pulls out a green baseplate and flips it over in his hands. "I guess we can start with this," he says.

I nod in agreement. "That can be the beach."

"Maybe we can build a tank, draw a Nazi flag on it."

"And then a plane for the Allies."

"And this—" He holds up a Lego man decked out in what looks like a superhero outfit. "He can be a parachuter."

I giggle, and his mouth curves up in a grin. I realize I've never seen him smile before, and I feel my cheeks grow warm when I find myself wishing he would smile more.

"But how are we going to tell a story?" I ask.

He frowns and glances in the toy chest, then pulls out a loose ball of yarn and begins unraveling it. "We can create a zipline from the plane down to the beach."

"And have him topple over the flag!" I exclaim, getting the idea.

"Good," a new voice says from behind us. We whirl around to see Mr. Berber leaning in the doorway, watching. "Your project's complete. Go grab some lunch."

Nathan and I exchange glances.

"But we didn't make anything yet," he says.

Mr. Berber walks towards us, crossing his arms. "Art isn't always brushstrokes and sculptures. That's what I want you kids to learn. Art is what you see, what you feel, what you create in the world around you." He nods towards the scattered Lego bricks between us. "Don't think I haven't seen the wall you've been building all year. It's why I paired you two up. Potential, that's what you have. And now, here you are, two opposing sides uniting to become friends and solve a problem. That kind of thing can break down barriers." He points to the newspaper cutout still on the chalkboard. "That kind of art can end wars."

Nathan stares at his hands, fiddling with the toy figure. I play with the plastic leaves of a palm tree.

"You both get an 'A,'" Mr. Berber says. He tilts his head towards the door. "Now come on. You've still got time for lunch before your next class."

"I'd like to do the project anyway," Nathan says quietly.

I glance at him, then nod. "Me, too."

Mr. Berber stops, a smile slowly spreading across his face like he's just confirmed something he's suspected all along. "Suit yourselves," he says. "I'll be at the easel if you need me."

A moment later, the first few notes of a rock song rises from the CD player at the front of the room. I glance at Nathan, then snap the palm tree on the plastic base and resume building the tank.

"I'm sorry I didn't do the project," I hear him say quietly. "My dad was sick. He, uh. He tends to get sick a lot around the holidays, you know? So I stayed home to make sure…"

His voice trails off. I stare at the bricks in my hand, lock another one into place.

"I was in the hospital," I tell him. "They did all sorts of tests, but they're still not entirely sure what's wrong with me. They think my cells… They don't function like other people's cells."

He holds up the Lego figure. "You mean like superhuman cells?"

"No, the opposite."

He's silent for a minute as he figures out what I mean. "Are you okay?"

I shrug. "Today I am."

"What about tomorrow?"

"I hope so."

"Yeah, me too," Nathan says. "It would suck to lose a friend."

I wish this is what happened. I wish Nathan and I had met all these years later in art class with a cool teacher named Mr. Berber who called us friends before we even knew that's what we were becoming. I wish our real friendship wasn't so fractured, that something like art could end this war—this division that exists between us, that's existed between us for years.

I wish we'd had this second chance.

But there's no use in wishing. Even if we met when we were fourteen, everything that came after would still be the same.

We still wouldn't have enough time.

Chapter Nine

"Lilac Sophia."

It's the way he says my name that makes me want to punch him. So I do—right in the arm.

"Ow! What the hell was that for?"

"Stop calling me that," I say.

"But that's your name."

"You know I changed it."

"You can't just change your name like that."

"Oh, no? Watch me."

We're standing at the end of my driveway, waiting for the bus to come. It's the second week of January, and we're bundled up in wool gloves and long scarves, but there's no snow on the ground. It hasn't snowed since Thanksgiving, even as the temperatures have dipped into the single digits and the weathermen call for snow flurries every other day. The wind is blowing cold, and I have to turn my back to keep my eyes from watering. Stubborn tears slip past my cheeks, and I hastily brush them away with the back of my glove. Nathan doesn't say anything. Maybe it's because his eyes are watering, too. Maybe it's because he knows I'll punch him again.

We're thirteen. At least, I'll be thirteen in a few more days. Five handwritten invitations to my birthday party are sitting in the front pocket of my backpack, waiting to be handed to my friends at lunch. Last year, my mom took me and Jessica Daley and Amanda Zeleski to the movies, but this year I'm having a sleepover where we'll play games and give each other makeovers and eat store-bought birthday cake right from the container with plastic forks. Then we'll talk about the boys at school, and I'll pretend to gag whenever someone mentions Nathan's name, and they'll ask if we can go next door and see if he wants to watch a movie with us, but I'll say no.

Nathan's not invited.

We look down the street at the same time, expecting the bus any minute now, but the bus is late. When I turn around, he's watching me, and for a second I see shades of the old Nathan. The Nathan who used to be my friend. It startles me because I don't expect it, and I open my mouth, wondering if I should say something, wondering if maybe I should see if he wants to watch a movie sometime like we used to when we were younger. But then he ducks his head and digs the tip of his sneaker into the fissure between sidewalk and grass. His dark hair has grown long, and it keeps falling into his eyes.

"You were up late last night," he says. I raise my eyebrows, and he hurries to explain. "I saw the light on in your room at, like, one in the morning."

"I fell asleep with it on," I say.

"Oh."

"Yeah."

"So, you weren't up finishing your art project for Mr. Molina's class?"

"No." I pause. "Were you?"

"I did it last week."

"Oh."

"Yeah."

Nathan's going to be a doctor. Either that or a paleontologist—something with bones. I guess whether the subject's living or extinct remains to be seen. When we were little, we'd spend hours in the creek behind our houses, burying model dinosaurs made out of balsa wood and then pretending to excavate them. One afternoon, a summer storm came on so suddenly, we had to abandon our dig site and race inside. His mother made us a snack of peanut butter and jelly squares, and we spent the rest of the afternoon sprawled on couch cushions on the floor watching cartoons, occasionally glancing out the window at the downpour, wondering what would become of our discoveries. When we met outside the next day, we couldn't remember where half the bones were buried. I'm pretty sure there's pieces of a Velociraptor still out there.

"Are you—" He cuts himself off abruptly and buries his face back in his scarf. I raise my eyebrows, and he shrugs. "You weren't in school last week."

"I had the flu."

He's looking at me like he wants to say more, like he wants to ask what he really wants to know. I should wait for him, extend this silence, force him to say something that makes me think he cares. But I don't.

"I'm fine," I answer for him. "I'm all better now."

He nods and lowers his eyes.

We hear the squeal of brakes as the bus approaches the stop sign on the corner. I exhale slowly and watch it turn down our street, my breath creating a cloud in the cold air.

"I like the name Lilac," I hear Nathan say as the bus rolls to a stop in front of us. The doors open with a hiss, and I reach for the metal railing. He's right behind me, his voice falling quiet so only I can hear.

"It sounds like springtime."

Chapter Ten

LILAC

They don't expect it when the fever finally breaks. They don't expect it when my labs come back within range. They don't expect it when I'm cleared to go home.

I've surprised them all.

That's right, I think smugly as I lower myself from the bed to the wheelchair.

I'm ninety-nine years old today. I'm gonna live to see a hundred.

Chapter Eleven

NATHAN

Jess's words have been haunting me all month. Everywhere I look now, it's like there's this lack of Lilac. She's not slouched in a chair in the auditorium, furiously dotting notes on index cards before school. She's not cursing at the combination on her locker and then throwing her hands in the air in defeat, wearing her jacket to first period because the bell has rung and she doesn't want to be late. She's not sitting in the corner desk in homeroom, flipping through the last pages of a book that wasn't assigned for English class—and I should know because I'm in her English class, and she's not there, either.

She's not here. And I don't get how suddenly I can feel her absence, how even when she was here and we weren't talking, the world still felt whole.

The cafeteria is buzzing with meaningless conversation. I amble over to the lunch line and grab a plastic yellow tray, loading it with a barely-edible cheeseburger, macaroni salad, chips, and a carton of chocolate milk. I hand over a few crumpled dollar bills, grab my change—

And stop.

I feel lost. Directionless. There's a crowd in front of me of people I've known since elementary school, and I wonder if I really recognize any of them. It all feels so...hollow. And why the hell is that?

"Mom says she's coming home today," Jess had said this morning at breakfast. She just raised her eyebrows, took another bite of Raisin Bran, then turned her attention to Jasper and that was that.

My eyes flick towards a round table near the windows. Amanda Zeleski and Jessica Daley are laughing and picking at their salads, an empty chair between them. I don't know why I'm surprised, like I expect her to be there now that Jess said she's coming home, but that chair is still empty, and the emptiness feels like a punch to the stomach. She should be there. She should be there, but she isn't.

"You waiting for the bus, Emery?" Dan bumps my shoulder and grins, then sidesteps me and makes his way over to our table where the rest of the track team is sitting.

I shake my head and plop a tray down beside him. I've got to knock it the hell off. I shouldn't be thinking about her like this. Lilac and I aren't friends, not anymore. She made that clear on plenty of occasions.

And yet...

How often did she meet my glance when we passed in the hallway because our lockers are right fucking across from each other? How often did she turn around during English class, her face filled with silent interest and something else, whenever I raised my hand to speak, and how many times did I offer a quick nod before averting my eyes, even as my heart squeezed at that something else I saw in hers.

Now she's coming home from the hospital, and where was I? Where have I been? Why couldn't I just find the fucking balls to go and see her?

After school, I vow to myself, stabbing at the macaroni salad with a plastic fork as my friends joke around me. After school, I'll stop at Mom's house—before he gets home—and tell her I'm okay, that I'm making the grades and I'm still on the team and I have a summer job lined up, and not to worry because this hasn't fucked up my life. Then I'll cross the lawn and climb the porch steps and reach for their doorknob like I've been doing practically my whole life, but I'll ring the doorbell instead because I've worn out that welcome.

I'll say hi to her mom.

I'll take the stairs two at a time.

I'll see my best friend.

Chapter Twelve

"What's Nathan doing on our front porch?" my mom asks as we pull into our driveway.

I lean forward and peer through the windshield, trying to get a closer look. "What the hell is he wearing is more like it."

Nathan sits up as soon as he sees us, lifts his hand in a wave, then leans to the side. My mom shifts the car into park, and we watch as he wraps his hands around the porch column and heaves himself to a standing position. My mother shakes her head and reaches for the purse at my feet.

"Do you need the wheelchair?" she asks.

"No, I'm good." I decide I can walk today. Besides, there's no way I'm going to confront this—whatever this is—unless I'm on a level playing field with him.

I slam the door shut behind me and lean against the hood of the car, waiting for my mom to go on ahead.

"Hello, Nathan," she says, failing to hide a smile as she passes.

"Hi, Mrs. Carpenter." He offers her a sheepish grin.

We stare at each other for a few moments. Down the block, the neighbor kids are doing tricks on their skateboards in the middle of the street. In the open garage across the way, Mrs. Willcox is unloading groceries from her car.

"So, I heard they were discharging you. Thought I'd come by and say hey."

"Nathan…" I say, eager to get to the more pressing question. "Why are you dressed as a giant hot dog?"

He glances down at the padded costume, then locks eyes with me, a grin spreading across his face. "See, here's the thing," he begins. "Dan asked me to cover for him at the hot dog stand down near the park, but I thought he meant actually serving hot dogs to, like, customers and stuff. Turns out, not so much."

I can't help it. I'm laughing so hard, there's a pain piercing my side and tears are gathering in my eyes. It's the most I've laughed in days—weeks, *months*—and seeing Nathan in a puffed-up hot dog costume is like letting the air out of a balloon that's been stretched too tight. Nathan holds me up by the forearms and waits while I struggle to catch my breath. There's a gleam in his eye when I finally swipe at the tears running down my cheeks.

"If you think that's funny, wait for this one—I can't get the damn thing off."

I'm howling again—so much that the earth begins to spin and before I know it, my knees are buckling to the grass. My mother hurries outside when she sees me on the ground and asks what's wrong, what happened, but all I can do is point and laugh some more.

"That's right," he says as my mother shakes her head and helps him out of the costume. "Laugh at my humiliation."

"I'm sorry, I'm sorry," I gasp, trying to gain control of my breathing.

"Good for you for being an entrepreneur, Nathan." My mother pats him on the shoulder and turns to go inside. "Lilac…" She taps her watch. "Ten minutes."

I lay on my back in the grass, arms outstretched. "Oh, my God," I say, exhausted from the exertion. "That's the best—the *best*."

"I'm so glad I can amuse you, Lilac Sophia."

"Did you at least get compensated for this torture?"

"He paid me."

"Yeah? How much?"

"Enough."

I sit up, leaning back on my elbows, and watch him cross to the porch, where he reaches for his sports bag. He's wearing a pair of red gym shorts and no shirt, and I feel a blush creeping into my cheeks when I realize how tan he is. I try to avert my eyes—try to look at the garage, the house, the sky—but my eyes keep falling back on him. He removes a t-shirt from the bag and pulls it over his head, his lips turning upwards into a smirk when he catches me looking.

"Shut up, Emery," I say, flopping back onto the grass.

It's a perfect spring day—one of those rare days where the sky is so brilliant and blue it seems endless, where the wind pushes the warm air out and you can finally breathe deep and clear. I watch a squirrel skip across branches in the canopy of the tree above me, watch the sunlight filter past the maple leaves. Then a shadow falls across my vision and something drops onto my chest.

"What's this?" I ask, sitting up.

"What's it look like?"

It looks like a bouquet of varying shades of lilacs, gathered and tied at the stems with a piece of twine. "But—"

Nathan's arm brushes mine as he stretches out next to me, hands tucked beneath his head, his gaze focused on the sky.

"I'm glad you're home," he says. I stare at the flowers, stare at him, at a loss for words. "It's never the same without you here."

Oh, how I wish this all was true.

Chapter Thirteen

LILAC

16 YEARS, 5 MONTHS

It's nighttime when we pull up to our house. The light from the garage is spilling onto the driveway, but the windows are dark, and everything seems so quiet and still. I imagine the squirrels are already nestled in the maple tree in the front yard, the neighbors down the block tucked away inside their beds. My mom shifts the car into park and reaches for the purse at my feet. I stare at the front porch, empty and waiting.

"Do you need the wheelchair?" she asks.

I nod. "Yeah. Yeah, I do."

She pops the trunk and heads to the back of the car. I glance up at the house next door. Their porch light is on, illuminating a splintering wooden bench and a planter full of pink impatiens. Through a break in the curtain on the side of the house, I can see the flickering blue light of a television set. I don't have to look up to his room to know the blinds are drawn.

My mom opens my door, holding me up by the forearms as I shift my weight and collapse into the wheelchair. The exertion is enough to make me have to catch my breath, and I lean forward and wait for the world to stop spinning.

"I'm sorry, I'm sorry," I say to my mom, but she shakes her head and strokes my hair.

"I'm just glad you're home." I close my eyes, knowing what words come next, hating myself for wishing they came from someone else. "It's never the same without you here."

Chapter Fourteen

LILAC

16 YEARS, 5 MONTHS

"Pst. Lilac."

My bedroom window is open a crack to usher in the fresh air, but that small inch of space is like a breach for my defenses. I can hear everything. I can hear the thud of his front door closing behind him, hear his cough as he crosses the yard, hear the scattering of dirt as he roots through the soil in the garden bed below, then hear thick pieces of mulch tapping against the windowpane at intervals.

I can hear him calling my name. His voice is hushed, but the words are clear and seem to vibrate with meaning.

"*Lilac Sophia.*"

I stare at the wall where a map of the world is riddled with red pushpins. All the places I want to go. All the places I've never been. Dozens of postcards decorate the space below it, held up with painter's tape. San Diego. Portland. New Orleans. Nashville. Welcome to somewhere, they all seem to say—where here is better than where you are.

And then his voice, pulling me back to this house, this room, this bed.

"See ya sometime, Lilac."
I close my eyes and roll over.
He's not really there, anyway.

Chapter Fifteen

NATHAN

I'm a shit.

I'm a shit, I'm a shit, I'm a little fucking shit.

I kick at the grass with the edge of my sneaker and palm my car keys, run my other hand across the back of my neck. Her window was open, and I thought… I thought…

I should have tried harder, shouted louder. I should be climbing up the porch steps right now, ringing their doorbell, bringing her a bouquet of her favorite flowers and stories from school.

I shouldn't be walking away from her window, shouldn't be headed in the direction of my mom's driveway, shouldn't be opening the door to my truck and starting the ignition.

I shouldn't be driving away.

Chapter Sixteen

I stumble up the cracked concrete steps to his apartment, follow him in through the front door. Almost thirty years old, and it still looks like a college dorm room—complete with a futon for a couch and a neon beer sign hanging on the wall.

Wait. No. I don't like this. I think it'll be too close to the truth. And, besides, if he's going to be a doctor, he should live in a high-rise or a brownstone in the city.

Let's try this again.

He lives in a brownstone on a street lined with birch trees, ankle-high fences set a foot apart from the trunks to keep Pomeranians and Pekinese from pissing on them as they pass. There's a Queen Anne loveseat in the front room and actual art above the fireplace—Cézanne, maybe. Or the abstract genius of Jackson Pollock. Nathan always did seem like a Jackson Pollock kind of guy.

We haven't seen each other in years, and he keeps glancing back at me to make sure I'm following him down the long hallway to the kitchen. He opens the fridge and pulls out a bottle of beer—something local, judging by the label—and holds it up in question. I nod, and he rifles through a drawer filled with extension cords and pens until he finds a bottle opener. We stand awkwardly on opposite sides of the island, separated only by a pile of bills and a bowl of ripened fruit. We glance around nervously—him looking at what's already familiar, me drinking in everything that's him.

He clears his throat and braces his hands on the marble countertop, his head bowed. It gives me an opportunity to study him—the way his hair still falls over his eyes, the way he still hunches slightly because he's always been on the taller side.

"What are you doing here?" he finally asks, meeting my eyes. His tone isn't cruel or accusing, but soft and rather like a plea, begging for the answers we never gave each other.

"I don't know," I say. "I mean, I could ask you the same thing. You're the one who showed up at my door—"

"I stopped in to get a cup of coffee at Starbucks," he interrupts. "That's hardly showing up at your door."

"It's where I work. It's where I've worked for five years now."

I don't know why I never dream bigger for myself. Maybe that's real life slipping past the wish. Maybe next time I need to make more of an effort, imagine I'm an art curator or a world-renowned researcher—something that matters to the fate of the world, something that creates a legacy, something that I want, if I'm honest with myself, even if it's barely believable. But there's no use wanting that now, so barista it is.

"I didn't know that," he says. "I had no idea you were here in the city. I would have called you."

"No, you wouldn't." I'm proud of myself for being so bold, for not letting him off the hook. But then I see him take a step back, like my words have stung, and I lower my eyes, scratch at the label on the beer bottle. "You wouldn't," I repeat, more softly now. "You'd call Jessica or Amanda, but you wouldn't call me." I nudge the bottle away. "It's okay. We were friends when we were kids, but we don't have to be friends now." I don't know what else to say, so I reach for my purse and turn to leave. "Thanks for the beer."

"Lilac Sophia…"

I still love the way he says my name.

"Lilac…"

I pause and close my eyes. The sound of that word— tender and strong—rolls around in my mind, reaching down into the pit of my stomach and clinging to the heart that's there. And then—

"I think I'm gonna be sick."

And I *am* sick—right across the bed, interrupting my daydream. My mom hears me retching and hurries into my bedroom, helps me into the bathroom while she strips the bed like she did when I was three and still believed in monsters who lived in closets. I wander back into my room and collapse into the plush chair by the closet door. Squeezing my eyes shut, I drag the hand-knit afghan from the back of the chair and wrap it around my shoulders to keep myself from shivering.

I'm not three today, I'm not three today…

"Do you need some water?" she asks.

"You want some water?" he says, but he's already filling a glass from the tap. He doesn't slide the glass across the counter like I expect him to. Instead, he walks around the kitchen island, so close my heart skips because I can smell the lingering remains of his cologne—or maybe it's just the scent of him. Our fingers brush, and he jerks away at the contact, though his eyes remain on my hand, like that touch has triggered some memory within him.

"You should—" His voice cracks, and he lifts his head and clears his throat and tries again. "Stay. You should stay. I've got a guest room upstairs. It's yours for the night if you want. We can order a pizza, spend the night catching up." He pauses. "I've missed you."

My breath hitches at his words, and when I meet his eyes, I can tell it's as true for him as it is for me. I don't know what to say. There's too much I want to say. A torrent of emotion is building inside of me, and I need to quiet the storm before I'm swept away.

I raise my eyebrow. "Spending the night? Isn't that a little forward, Emery?"

He chuckles, his shoulders relaxing. The storm has passed.

"Come on, Lilac," he says. "Your bedroom was directly across from mine for over a decade. I've already seen everything."

"You wish," I retort, but my cheeks are still burning.

I stay.

Chapter Seventeen

LILAC

"Here's some ginger ale and chicken soup."

Bless my mother. She tries to be helpful. I think she really believes I can be cured by ginger ale and chicken soup. If only it were that easy. I'd take ginger ale and chicken soup over this cocktail of medicines they try to feed me any day.

She puts the bed tray down on the nightstand beside me and helps me sit up, securing the pillows behind my back. Then she settles the tray across my lap, and I notice there's a chocolate pudding cup in the corner. I stare at it for a moment, a lump growing in my throat. These are the little gestures that matter now, when maybe I wouldn't have paid attention before. I blink back tears and reach for the cup before I let the moment consume me.

"Allison called," my mother says, taking a seat in the chair by the closet. She watches me for a moment as I struggle to tear open the lid, then gets up to do it for me. I lick the lid clean, then dip the spoon in and scoop up a thick, chocolatey glob.

"Why, did she want to tell you about the new toilet they picked out for their bathroom? I bet Kurt wanted a bidet."

My mom's mouth twitches, and I know she's trying to hold back a smile. "She called to see how your trip home from the hospital was." Then she adds, "And they're putting the new flooring down in the kitchen."

Allison is my sister—ten years older and everything I'll never be. She and her new husband moved to Phoenix at the beginning of the year after his company sent him to the other side of the country to oversee their financial operations. But she calls my mom every day to ask about a chicken recipe our grandma used to make or to talk about a new natural cleaning product she read about in a magazine. Her latest calls have been about the renovations she and Kurt are making to their 1960s ranch house. Last week, she spent an hour on the phone describing four different vanities, saying she couldn't decide and needed a second opinion. My mom says she secretly wants to know how I'm doing without being a pest, but I don't think that's it. She never asks to speak to me.

"What did you tell her?"

"That you settled in nicely."

That's my mom. Always trying to put a positive spin on shitty situations.

"That's great," I say, not bothering to hide my sarcasm. "So, when are you going to pick them up from the airport?"

My mom's mouth pulls down in a frown, and she narrows her eyes. I know that look. It's the same look she used to give me when I was little and digging up fake dinosaur bones in the creek out back—that look that says enough with the attitude.

"You know they're both still settling in at their jobs, Lilac," my mom gently reproaches.

I wonder if it's the fact that I'm stuck in bed like this that's keeping her from yelling at me. No use grounding me now, right? I've already got a life sentence.

"And the renovations and the cost of flights…" she continues. "You know they'll come visit as soon as they can."

I sigh and shove a spoonful of pudding in my mouth. My mom wants to believe that, I'm sure, but the truth is I've never been close with my sister. Which is why I don't think it's just her job and the house and the cost of anything that's keeping her away.

Outside, a car door slams. Mom cranes her neck to peek out the window. "Oh, there's Mrs. Emery. I've got to get her casserole dish back to her."

"Ham and broccoli again?"

"It was better than the tuna—her cooking might be improving. You'll be okay for a minute?"

"Yes," I say, trying to keep the annoyance from my voice as I scrape the last of the pudding from the snack cup. "I will be okay for a minute."

My mom frowns and hurries out the door. A few seconds later, I hear the front door open and close, then the muffled sound of her voice as she hurries across the side yard.

It's springtime—my favorite season. I imagine daffodils and crocuses peeking through fresh-spread mulch in the garden bed below my window, imagine the creek behind my house filling up from the overnight rains. Soon the afternoons will be bursting with newly-licensed classmates going for joyrides in their parents' cars, windows rolled down and music blaring from car stereos, but now the world is quiet, like it's getting ready to exhale after a long, bleak winter.

I twist my neck to look out the window. Mom and Mrs. Emery are chatting in the driveway next to Nathan's truck. *Nathan's truck.*

His window is directly across from mine, and I can't help but sneak a glance. The blinds are up but the curtains are drawn—a purple-patterned atrocity his mom put up the day Nathan moved out. I wonder what they turned it into—a guest room, maybe, like my parents did when Allison moved in with Kurt. Or maybe an exercise room. Mrs. Emery has become a jogger over the years—or so my mother says. I didn't quite believe her until I saw her for myself on the day we arrived home from the hospital.

The first time.

She was wearing Lycra running shorts and had her short hair pushed back with a lime green hairband. In her hands were small, magenta-colored weights to show the world she meant business.

"Nice for John," my dad had commented, watching her in the rearview mirror for way longer than was necessary. "Maybe he'll stick around more often now."

My mom had raised her eyebrows and shifted in her seat to look at him. He'd glanced at her, a smile spreading on his face. "Don't worry, honey. I'm not going to leave you just because—"

"Just because what?"

Just because he was already banging his accountant.

I think I'd like to go back to being three today. At least when there's a monster in the closet, you can always shut the door.

Chapter Eighteen

There was a time when we were a real family. I swear, this is true.

My mother worked part-time as a staff writer for the local newspaper, which meant she was home by three o'clock every day to see me off the bus while Allison stayed behind at school for marching band or student council. I remember sitting at the kitchen counter, finishing my math worksheets while I watched my mom cook dinner— pork chops with rice or meatloaf and green beans or my favorite, fish tacos. At exactly five-thirty, we'd hear the hum of the garage door and two seconds later the slam of car doors. My dad would come in first, carrying his briefcase and jacket in one hand and loosening his tie in the other, and Allison would follow, backpack slung over one shoulder and a pile of books in the crook of her arm. They'd drop their things on the stools next to me and then ask what was for dinner, and Mom would scold them both and tell them to wash up first—it was Family Night.

Every night was family night back then.

Funny how quickly that can change.

I'm seven years old when Allison announces she's going out with friends instead of spending Friday night eating pizza and playing board games with us. Mom and Dad exchange glances, like they knew this was coming only they weren't ready for it—or maybe they thought it would happen sooner or even not at all.

Allison is a black and white kind of person—there are no shades of gray with her. My parents say that from an early age she decided to follow the rules and that was that: bedtime at eight, always clear your plate, homework before play. That's who she is—whoever she decides to be, whatever she sets her mind to, she goes full-throttle for it. Which is why, when she announces that she's going to the arcade with friends instead of staying for family game night, my parents raise an eyebrow but don't say a word. Their sighs of resignation indicate it's about time she decided to be a teenager. They should know there's no stopping her, anyway. This is who she wants to be now.

This is seventeen.

"Mind telling me who these friends are?" Dad asks as Nathan and I shout that there's a car turning down our street. We've been charged with keeping an eye out for the pizza delivery, and we're taking the job very seriously.

My dad reaches in his back pocket for his wallet.

"You already know all my friends, Dad," Allison protests. "You've known them since we were all in diapers."

"He's here, he's—Oh. Never mind," Nathan says. "That's just Mr. Willcox."

My dad frowns and takes a twenty out of his wallet anyway, as if that will save him the hassle of yet another false alarm. Then, on second thought, he pulls out another ten and holds it out to Allison.

"Home by eleven."

"Eleven-thirty!" my mom calls from the kitchen.

"What your mother said," he says with a wink. Allison grins, kisses him on the cheek, and runs out the door. "You two." Dad points to us and crooks his finger. "Let's go. Help me set up this game."

"But we have to wait for the pizza!"

"The pizza will get here without you watching for it."

"Not in thirty minutes or less it won't."

My dad chuckles and ruffles Nathan's hair. "Don't be a smart aleck," he says, and though Nathan ducks away, he's grinning.

The pizza arrives in twenty-six minutes.

In another four minutes, we're gathered around the coffee table in the living room, paper plates piled high with pepperoni pizza, drink cups full of cola.

"I want to be the red car!"

"Fine, I'll be green."

"Here, Dad, put your peg person in the car."

"Who's going first?"

"Lilac, stop fanning yourself with the bills."

"But I'm rich!"

"Nice spin, Nate. Let's see where you land."

"'Make new friends.' But I don't wanna make new friends."

Conversations overlap as we settle in to play *The Game of Life*, but we barely get through my turn when the doorbell rings. Mom and Dad glance at each other. I'm already off the floor and running to the front door.

"Hi, Mrs. Emery."

"Lilac." A frown creases Mrs. Emery's face, her eyes drawn with worry. "Is Nathan—Oh, you are here. Good." She glances over my shoulder into the living room, her shoulders sagging when she sees her son sitting on the floor, chewing on a pizza crust.

"Hi, Mom."

My mom transfers her plate from her lap to the game board and pushes the coffee table aside so she can stand. "You didn't tell her you were here?" she asks Nathan. "I'm sorry, Joanne, I thought you knew he was staying for dinner."

"I had to put in overtime at work," Mrs. Emery explains. "But then I get a call from John saying Nathan never came home after school."

"But I did go home! I told Dad—"

"Get your things and let's go," Mrs. Emery says sternly. Nathan stares at her. Something passes between them in a split second—something I don't understand. Mrs. Emery softens, her voice growing more tender. "I need you home now, Nate," she says quietly.

Nathan sighs. Whatever it was they said without speaking has changed him. Right now, in this moment, he's no longer my goofy friend who jokes around with my dad, no longer the boy who's always ready for a smile or a laugh. Now he's more subdued, like something has fallen silent within him, burying who he really is beneath.

"It's okay," I tell him because I don't know what else to say to bring him back. "We'll leave everything where it is and play tomorrow."

Nathan gets to his feet slowly, wordlessly. He doesn't even look at me, but he grabs the crust off my plate and stuffs it in his mouth like that will keep him from saying something he shouldn't.

"Got your backpack?" Mrs. Emery asks, resting a hand on his shoulder.

"No," Nathan says and trudges past her out the door. "Because I already went home today."

My mom closes the door behind them and glances at my dad. I run back into the living room and kneel in front of the coffee table, gathering up my pile of money for safekeeping.

"It's okay," I repeat, tucking Nathan's money beneath the game board. "We'll just leave everything where it is and play again tomorrow, right?" I look up. "Right, Dad?"

"Actually, kiddo, I have to go into work tomorrow."

"But it's Saturday."

"It's Saturday, Frank." My mother stands on the other side of the couch and crosses her arms. For a second it feels like the couch is a shield between them, creating a wall only I can see. I want to sit on the cushions between them. I want to jump over the back of the couch and pull my dad along with me as if to prove that this barrier can be broken.

"Yep. I know." My dad's voice is light, but he holds my mom's stare. "But the end of the month reports won't write themselves."

"Your end of the month reports can wait one weekend while you're with your family." My mother grits her teeth. I stare down at the game board, a colorful path filled with choices: School. Career. Relationships. Family.

I wonder which my father is choosing now.

"Who is it this time, Frank?" My mother's voice is barely above a whisper, but I hear her. Of course I hear her.

I watch him stand and cross into the kitchen.

"Leave it alone, Evelyn," he says. "It's Family Night."

He could tear down that wall if he wanted to. It would only take a few words, maybe a gesture or two. But instead he's laying bricks one by one.

My dad is building a fortress. And none of us are allowed in.

Chapter Nineteen

A social gathering. That's what my best friend Kate calls it when she says she's inviting a few people over to the apartment later. Just a couple of pizzas and some cheap beer for a low-key Friday night hangout with friends. Surprisingly, given her track record for out-of-control parties over the years, low-key is exactly what it turns out to be.

"I'm twenty now," she says with a shrug. "All that other stuff gets old."

We're twenty now, living in an old Victorian house three blocks away from campus that's been converted into multiple apartments, thanks to the local real estate tycoon's talent for taking advantage of students' desperate need to get out of the crowded dorms. Our attic apartment runs the length of the house, with two bedrooms barely big enough to fit a bed and a dresser, a bathroom the size of a closet, and a narrow kitchen we've turned into study space because neither of us like to cook, anyway.

Kate wrinkled her nose the first time she saw it, but I fell in love with this place from the start, and every time I walk through the door, I fall in love with it again. Not just because of the built-in bookcases nestled beneath the eaves near our royal blue garage sale couch, or the second-hand rugs we've thrown haphazardly across the wood floors, or even the life-sized glass mosaic Kate decided to create on the brick columns so we'll never get our security deposit back. It's not the curtains we made out of tablecloths, or my grandpa's old military trunk we use as a coffee table, or the ivy plant on top of the fridge given to us by Kate's parents that we haven't managed to kill just yet. It's none of it. It's all of it.

It's the fact that this is ours.

Kate's art major friends are sprawled across the sofa and lounging on throw pillows on the floor when I walk through the door after my shift at the pizza shop downtown. This is okay, this job. I don't mind it. I'm only twenty, anyway—just a college student trying to dream bigger for herself.

I like being twenty. It feels like a comfortable number—a number of possibilities. On the one hand, I'm no longer a child. On the other hand, I'm a heartbeat away from being an adult. It's like everything is ending and beginning in the same breath, and I can experience both in this in-between. A new decade. A new life. I can start over, I can be taken seriously in this world. Soon I can be anything I choose to be, do anything I want to do. But I'm only twenty now and still in college.

So Lou's Pizza it is.

The pink and orange paper lanterns we've strung across the ceiling cast a cozy glow around the apartment, and I kick off my sneakers by the front door, happy to be home and even happier to see Kate was true to her word and whatever gathering she did have here has at least dwindled to a handful of friends hanging out in our living room. They all seem content enough to be talking among themselves and watching whatever movie is playing on the TV. I cross to the kitchen and toss a container on the table next to some of Kate's art supplies and my biology textbook.

"Appetizers for whoever wants them," I announce.

One of the guys jumps up from his place on the floor and flips open the lid. He takes a bite of a cold mozzarella stick and grins. "Thanks, Lila."

"You can thank the customer who never picked up their order," I tell him.

Kate steps up beside me. "Long night?"

"Long week," I admit. I glance around at the empty beer bottles littering the floor and table. Kate nudges my arm and holds hers out with a wink, and I gratefully accept and tilt it back.

And freeze.

"Please don't be mad," she whispers beside me.

Familiar dark brown eyes lock on mine, neither of us daring to move, both of us wondering who will give in first.

"He's our neighbor," Kate pleads, her tone hushed but urgent. "I ran into Dan on the stairs and invited them both before I realized what I was saying—you know how I get. And besides. They brought the beer."

I glance down at the bottle I'm holding, then shove it back into Kate's hands. "It doesn't matter." I grab my textbook off the table. "I'm going to bed."

I can feel his eyes on me as I pass him and climb the slight step-up into my bedroom. The sliding door's been off track for weeks, and I mentally curse my landlord because from my place on the bed, I have the perfect view of the living room—and of him.

Nathan.

Bacteria. I need to focus on bacteria. Spirochetes and mycoplasma—and I can't help it that my eyes keep drifting over the top of my textbook to meet his. He lifts his beer bottle to his lips and glances at me, pauses when he sees me looking at him. Our eyes lock. I can't tell what he's thinking. I don't want to know what he's thinking.

I roll over to face the wall. From here, I can see the full moon, perfectly shaped by the small, round pivot window. It casts a shadow across the carpet where the light refuses to reach, and I put my book down to mentally trace the path it creates—past my CD player and along my dresser to where a childhood lamp sits in the dark. I grab a wool sweater off the end of the bed and quickly throw it over the lamp to cover it.

"You don't want to join the party?"

I jump and whirl around like I've been caught, but he doesn't even glance at the sweater on the dresser or what's hiding beneath it. He's standing in the doorway, staring at me like he wants to say something more—like he wants to cross this divide that's between us, only he doesn't know how.

It's fine with me. He can stay on the other side of whatever barriers we've built forever for all I care.

I hold up the book and try to focus on the text, but the words swim because he's just so *there*.

"You'd rather be reading—" Nathan steps into my room and takes the book from me, ignoring my protests. He flips it around so he can read the title. "*Bacteria and the Body: An Analysis of Human Microbiota*." He raises an eyebrow. "Fascinating."

"It's for class," I tell him.

It's because I'm going to be a doctor. I decide this when I'm fourteen, even though I don't tell anyone. It's part of my bargain with God: He saves my life, I save everyone else's.

Except, that's real life. And in real life, God doesn't seem to be holding up his end of the deal very well.

Nathan hands the book back to me. He opens his mouth to speak, then closes it again, like he's still not sure what he wants to say.

"Come on, you two!" Kate calls from the living room. I glance behind Nathan to see they've pushed some of the furniture out of the way and now all her friends are gathered in a circle on the floor. Kate holds up an empty beer bottle and dances it in the air. "We're playing Spin the Bottle!"

I glance at Nathan. The corner of his mouth lifts up.

"Oh, hell no," I say and slide off the bed. I reach for the sweater on my dresser and squeeze past him, past Kate's friends, and across the apartment where I grab my sneakers by the laces and hurry out the door.

"Lilac—Lilac! Hold up!"

He's on the stairs behind me, but I ignore him and speed up—past the mailboxes and bikes and skateboards locked on a rack in the foyer and out onto the porch where I inhale the cold night air.

Large white bulbs line the edge of the roof and over-sized ferns hang from hooks as if to make the house look classier than it really is by hiding the peeling paint and splintering wood and the fact that this might have been a nice family home once, but it's only a temporary shelter for an ever-rotating group of students now. There's an ashtray with cigarette butts in the far corner, and an empty beer can is hidden behind the drooping leaves of one of the ferns.

"Lilac."

"Just go home, Nathan," I say. "Go home to your apartment or go back to the party. I don't care, just leave me alone."

The screen door creaks. I hear the wooden floorboards give against his weight as he steps onto the porch.

"Do you go home?" he asks. "Back to the house on Peachtree, I mean. Holidays and breaks and all that?"

I glance over my shoulder at him. "Of course. It's my home. Don't you?"

He shrugs, and I turn around and study him. When I found out we were going to the same school, I scheduled all my classes to make sure I could avoid him. When I found out we were living in apartments only one floor apart, I timed my exits and entries so I'd never have to see him. When I went home for winter break, I kept an eye on his driveway for his truck so I could make sure we never ran into each other. But I guess that was all for nothing. He was never there.

"Wait, you don't go home to see your parents for break?"

"Not if I can help it."

"What about Christmas?" I ask. "You were here for Christmas?"

"I went to Dan's for a few days."

"But you love your Christmas traditions."

"No," he corrects me. "I love *your* Christmas traditions."

This stuns me silent. I think back on all those times he came over to help us string popcorn for the tree. All those Christmas Eves he spent with me on the couch watching

Rudolph the Red-Nosed Reindeer on TV. All those early mornings when we would meet across the yards and tell each other what Santa brought us and then, when we stopped believing in Santa—before we stopped believing in each other—we'd exchange gifts ourselves.

He shrugs and ducks his head, scrapes the sole of his sneaker against the edge of the welcome mat. And I know what he's thinking. *It's not that you can't go home. It's that you don't always want to.*

"You should have told me," I say quietly.

He shakes his head. "And what would you have done? Invite me home with you? Come on, Lilac," he scoffs. "Your family is just as fucked up as mine."

I feel like I've been slapped in the face. I guess that's what happens when someone throws a heavy dose of reality at you.

"My dad—"

"Is just as big of an asshole as my father. It's okay. You can say it. Parents are human."

But I don't want to say it. Not here, not now. Not to him.

"My dad tries his best."

"Your dad doesn't try at all. Lilac, how many times did we meet outside like this in the middle of winter to complain about our parents when we were kids?" He takes a step closer. I take a step back. "How many times did you have to pretend you weren't crying when he missed the school play or science fair or another family game night? And then he'd be there on your birthday with some great present like that would make up for it. Our parents were shit parents, Lilac."

"Not my mom," I interrupt him angrily. "Don't you dare say that about my mom."

He lifts his hands in defense. "No, not your mom. And maybe not my mom, either. But maybe—"

"Don't you dare blame her, Nathan Emery." I can feel hot tears beginning to sting my eyes. "After the hell my mom's been through, don't you dare blame her."

He goes quiet at that. He takes a step towards the railing, puts his hands in his pockets and stares out at the quiet street. Down the road to the left, all the businesses are closed up for the night. To the right, houses are darkened. It feels like we're the only ones in the world who are awake right now, and it makes me feel close to him. I quickly sit on the porch step.

I don't want to feel close to him.

I pull my sweater on over my head, unable to escape the chill that's begun to set in. Nathan keeps his gaze focused straight ahead. There's nothing there. Just a street followed by another yard and a house. It's just a blackness. A nothingness. But I know that's not what he's seeing.

"I don't understand how you can forgive him," he says, his voice quiet. "I wish I knew how you do it. Because maybe then…"

I look up sharply. "You think I forgive him? He made a vow to my mom—'til death do us part.' I mean, I guess I'm fulfilling that part of the equation for them, right?" I shake my head, trying to stop the words from spilling out because I don't want to be saying this to him—not now, not here—but everything's coming up too much, too fast. "Where is he? Where the hell is he, Nathan? He's not here when I need him, and I don't want to have to do this on my own. I shouldn't have to do this on my own. I'm sixteen years old and I'm dying, and it shouldn't be like this! It was never supposed to be like this. Not now. Not yet…"

Oops. That's real life slipping past again. Funny how I can only seem to say what I'm really feeling to Nathan.

And not even the real Nathan at that.

"I think sometimes I hate him." I'm back where I belong again—on the porch step of a rundown house in the middle of winter. "Allison got all that time with him when he was still a dad, and I don't know how much time I have left and he's barely here. And I don't know what to do with that. I don't know what I can do but hate him for it."

I look up at him. He's staring down at me, and I swear his eyes are glistening beneath the porch lights.

"I want to go home," I tell him. "To the home I had before."

He draws in a breath and turns, focusing again on the nothingness. "I wish I could be sure that ever existed."

Chapter Twenty

NATHAN

My sister's dinner party is nothing fancy. Just pork chops, brown rice, and a salad with something that looks like lettuce and tries to act like lettuce but definitely isn't lettuce. But we're eating in the dining room because of ambiance—whatever that's supposed to mean—and for reasons made clear only to her, Jess is insisting on using what she calls her "good china"—a set that once belonged to a grandmother I barely knew.

I didn't question her when she claimed the china for herself after our grandmother died and my mom inherited items from the estate, didn't question her when she made me go hunting in the basement for it this morning, even though they look just like regular dishes to me. I didn't even question her when she spent half an hour rearranging a floral centerpiece, wondering every five minutes if she needed to add more daisies. But when she asked me to polish the silverware, I told her she was a lunatic. Even Tim took her by the shoulders and said maybe she was going a tad overboard.

"I just want everything to be perfect!" she wailed.

"It's just Mom, Jess," I told her. "You can put out paper plates and plastic forks, and the only thing she would care about is the latest crap in Jasper's pants."

Jasper heard his name and started giggling, which caused Tim to chuckle, which led to Jess throwing down the salad tongs and storming off into the living room to fluff the couch cushions or something.

An hour later, I was polishing the silverware.

An hour after that, she had placed herself strategically behind Jasper, shielding herself from the death glares I was shooting her. Mom was on the floor next to Jasper's playmat, pointing out pictures of cows and chickens in one of the dozen new books she brought with her. Tim was sitting on one end of the couch.

My dad was on the other.

"This was a bad idea," I watched Tim lean down and whisper to Jess.

He was right. This was a horrible, no good, terrible idea.

Jess shooed him away and avoided my attempts at ESPing how pissed I was at her. Tim, at least, had the decency to shoot me an apologetic shrug. I couldn't blame him. Jess, on the other hand…

"And what does the farmer say to the chicken?"

I snorted. "I have a few suggestions."

"Okay!" Jess clapped her hands. "Time for dinner!"

And that's how we all ended up here in the dining room, steeped in awkward silence, staring at an overcrowded bouquet of daisies while pork chops grew cold on my deceased grandmother's china.

"Dinner is delicious, Jessica," my mother says.

You'd think that's a fair attempt at conversation, beginning at least ten minutes' worth of comments on recipes and the floral centerpiece and the china, but instead she turns her attention back to Jasper.

Way to hide behind a one-year-old, Mom.

I sit in silence and push the lettuce-that-isn't-lettuce around with my fork, listening to my mother and Jess make airplane noises for Jasper while intermittently asking questions about Tim's latest business acquisition. My dad is sitting across from me, eyes fixed on his own plate, his right hand wrapped around his glass of water like he and the glass will both shatter to pieces if he lets go.

So. This is just as uncomfortable for him as it is for me. Good.

God, I wish I was anywhere but here right now. How the hell did Jess rope me into this, anyway? I should have hightailed it over to Jamie's at the very mention of dinner, should have gone to Dan's with a pizza in hand so we could spend hours avoiding life by playing video games in his basement, should have run next door to Lilac's—

My fork slips from my hand, and I recover by reaching for my own glass and chugging down my water, giving me time to think and avoid my sister's raised brow.

Lilac. Where the hell did that thought come from? And why is she suddenly everywhere? She haunts the hallways at school, lingers in the empty chair in the cafeteria at lunch, lives in my memories like they happened yesterday. How long has it been since I crossed the yard between our houses for pizza and board games? How long has it been since we stood together at the bus stop, since we exchanged even a few measly words?

Something weird is happening to my heart, turning it inside out, and I clear my throat and shove a forkful of definitely-not-lettuce in my mouth and focus on chewing.

"How's school?"

At first, I don't think he's talking to me, and when I look up, my dad is still looking at his plate, making me wonder if maybe I actually imagined it. But a second later, his eyes flick up to meet mine before turning away again.

"School's school," I say, not bothering to keep my annoyance a secret. I might have to be in the same room as him, but that doesn't mean I have to talk to him.

"Nate made the honor roll again."

"That's wonderful, Nathan!" my mom exclaims. "Why didn't you tell me?"

I remain silent, scoop up some rice with my fork and shovel it into my mouth.

"You should tell your mother these things," my dad says.

"Why, because she's so concerned for my welfare?"

A hand slams down on the table, rattling the china. It startles Jasper enough that he starts to cry, but I'm not surprised. I knew this was coming. I could have called it from the minute they all stepped through the door tonight.

It's what he says next that catches me off-guard.

"That's enough, Nathan." The words are sharp, but my dad's face looks tired, defeated. I don't care. I'm not here to have sympathy for him. "We've put up with this behavior for months, and now it's time to come home."

I can't believe what I'm hearing. No, I mean—I *really* can't believe what I'm hearing.

"For months? You've put up with my behavior for months. That's rich. How about years, Dad, huh? How about seventeen years? How about that?" I drop my fork on the plate and push my chair back. "This is bullshit."

"Nate, please," Jess says, rocking a wailing Jasper against her shoulder.

"No, this is bullshit, Jess." I open my mouth again, start to tell her she's just as much a part of the problem as everyone else because what did she do but hide behind clubs and college and her family while I was at home picking up the pieces? But what's the point in bringing all of that up now. What's the point of any of this now.

They're all talking at once. Jess is pleading and Tim is reaching for Jasper and Mom and Dad are alternating between speaking to me and yelling at each other, and I don't care. I just don't care.

I stand up.

I walk out.

My dad was right about one thing. It was time to go home.

I just wish I knew where the hell that was.

Chapter Twenty-One

I'm six months old. People are saying words I don't understand and when I try to talk, they just nod and pat my head, but they're not listening, they're not listening, they're not listening. I want to scream.

So I do.

Chapter Twenty-Two

FIVE MONTHS EARLIER

I may have never been close with my sister, but I like to think I still know her pretty well. Which is why I know that when Kurt finally proposes to her on a romantic stroll along the beach, she immediately starts envisioning delicate wedding bouquets made of roses and calla lilies and elegant bridal gowns adorned with lace and pearls because that's who Allison is. She wants everything to be perfect, and everything is perfect because that's also who Allison is. She gets the venue she wants on the date she wants for the price she wants.

The only problem is me.

No one expects me to not be there when she has her magic moment trying on her first wedding dress. But I'm not. I'm too busy having a seizure that lands me in the hospital with a father who doesn't know what to do, so he calls my mom. So my mom's not there, either.

And the night of her bachelorette party? Nope. Still absent, thanks to the fact that my stomach decides to revolt every time I try to sip so much as chicken broth, and I'm too weak to get out of bed. You'd think my dad would love to be there to clean up that mess, but he takes off on a business trip to Portland and leaves the caregiving to my mom.

My dad's a middle-manager for a flooring company. There are no business trips to Portland.

Allison never says anything—what can she say to a sick sister that doesn't make her sound like a horrible, selfish person? But I can hear it in her voice every time she stops over to share her big book of wedding plans with my mom. Disappointment. Resentment. I'm disrupting her vision. I'm the hitch in the perfect plan, making everything fall apart.

Only, it's not just Allison's wedding I'm disrupting. That's just the tipping point. It's my dad's shiny new post-divorce life where he can no longer pretend everyone is happy and healthy and well by ignoring what's right in front of him. It's my former friendship with Nathan, a reminder of what we once were to each other rising up from the ashes because he's right next door and there's no avoiding each other.

Worlds are colliding now. The past is catching up to the present, collapsing around me into the black hole known as my future.

Unraveling without end.

Chapter Twenty-Three

Today's graduation day. Exclamation points! Squeals of joy! Hugs and kisses and all that other crap that's supposed to mark the end of one chapter and the start of another. I don't know. Sometimes I think it'd be easier just to close the book altogether and start fresh by picking a story you'd actually want to read. At least then you can pretend you had some say in the matter, no matter how it turns out in the end.

But what do I know. My book's already been written, and I know how it turns out.

We're in the cafeteria putting on our robes, small groups of friends crowding around the same tables they've eaten lunch at for the past four years. There's a can of hairspray and a spattering of bobby pins on the table near Jessica and Amanda, where they're helping some of the theater kids straighten their caps. I spy Nathan across the room, surrounded by the track team. When he catches me looking, he smiles, claps one of them on the shoulder, then makes his way over.

"Big day," I say because I guess that's the kind of thing you're supposed to say on days like today.

Nathan chuckles like he can tell what I'm really thinking. "Did you get your yearbook?"

"Not yet. I'll pick it up after."

"Better idea," he says, placing a hand on my elbow and spinning me around. "Let's pick it up now."

Before I know it, we're zipping through the crowd, barely pausing to exclaim, "Oh, my God, can you believe this day is finally here?" to classmates as we pass. There's a table by the exit stacked with yearbooks. My English teacher from ninth grade looks up as we approach.

"Lila," she greets me with a smile. "I was wondering when you'd be stopping by." She glances down at a sheaf of papers in front of her and checks off my name, then reaches into a canvas bag by her chair and pulls out a yearbook. I don't question it. Weirder things have happened in this school.

"Thanks, Mrs. G.," I say as the principal claps his hands and shouts for everyone to get in line for the procession.

"Two lines all the way to the football field," he's calling over the clamor of a dozen conversations. "Please make sure the tassels are on the right side of your cap!"

Nathan looks down at me, excitement etched on his face. "This is it. Catch ya later, Lilac."

In a second, he's gone.

The space where he was just standing seems hollow without him, and I don't know what to do with that—or with the yearbook I'm now holding in my hands. A teacher ushers me into line. I tuck the yearbook under my arm and hope the long sleeves of the commencement gown covers it up.

The afternoon sun is starting to set by the time we begin filing onto the track. It feels like only minutes ago that I was walking through the doors to the cafeteria, cap and gown in hand, waiting to graduate with the rest of my classmates, and now the moment's come so soon. It's funny how time passes like that—swift one minute, forever the next.

There's a crowd in the stands, and I can't help but glance up, scanning the faces for my family. When I see them, I wave with my free hand and grin. Mom, Dad, and Allison are sitting with the Emerys, Nathan's two older sisters and their families taking up the rest of the row beside them.

I'm seated between Christine Blythe and Emmalyn Caster in uncomfortable white folding chairs that make us all pray to whatever god wants to listen that the ceremony will be a short one. But up on the stage, our principal is talking about pride and what it means to be a scholar and the benefits of a fine education, reciting anecdotes about dream chasers and how now it's our turn.

I hear someone whisper my name, feel a tap on my shoulder. When I turn around, Nathan is sitting diagonally from me, leaning forward to get my attention.

"Did you open your yearbook yet?"

"What? No," I hiss over my shoulder. "What are you doing? You're not even supposed to be in that row."

"I switched seats. Check out your yearbook." He ducks down to grab the book from under my chair, resulting in a "Come on, man!" from the boy behind me and a glare from Christine beside me.

"Switch seats with me," I whisper to her.

"No way."

But I'm already standing up, mere seconds away from drawing attention to ourselves and causing a scene. "We'll trade back when we stand for our diplomas," I explain, gesturing for her to scoot over. Christine rolls her eyes and sighs and slides into my seat. I plop the yearbook in my lap.

Behind me, Nathan grins and leans forward, his arms resting on the back of my chair. I can feel his breath rustling my hair, sending a chill down the back of my spine. I open the book and look at the inside cover, expecting it to be blank and eagerly awaiting empty messages from friends that may never come, but instead it's bursting with writing. I fan through the rest of the pages. Messages and quotes and memories are scrawled in black ink on autograph pages, in the margins, across the hardbound covers. I inhale softly. I recognize the handwriting. They're all from Nathan.

I turn to look at him, open my mouth to speak, but the words won't come. He's sitting back in his chair, staring forward like he's busy concentrating on the valedictorian's speech, but there's a smile curling up the corner of his lips.

"What is this?" I ask him. He winks but doesn't say anything. I turn to the boy beside him, who's nodding his head along to the music streaming from his headphones. "Switch with me."

He looks up. "Oh, come on."

But I'm already out of my seat, leaning my chair forward so I can step into the aisle behind me.

"I'm not accepting your diploma for you," he says, dutifully trading places.

Nathan is grinning now, and though his eyes are focused straight ahead, I see his chest rise and fall with stifled laughter.

"Making quite the commotion, aren't you, Lilac?"

"What is this?" I ask again.

"Keep going."

So I do. I turn the page, begin scanning the pictures for familiar faces before I realize they're all familiar—they're all of us, me and Nathan. Us at the tenth-grade bonfire, us concentrating on our chemistry experiment, us at the ninth-grade homecoming dance. We're there as kids—our first bus ride, him clutching a Superman lunchbox, and our first time learning how to ride a two-wheel bike. We're there for holidays and neighborhood picnics and posing in our Ghostbusters costumes for Halloween. We're there on every page, our life together captured in perfect snapshots.

But how? Why?

I feel hot tears begin to gather at the corner of my eyes, and I keep my head bowed, try to blink them away. I sneak my hand into his, and he raises it to his lips.

"Last page," he whispers.

I turn the page, stare speechlessly at the words I didn't think I'd ever hear. Nathan squeezes my hand, and when I look up, his eyes are shining, filled with earnest and everything he could ever hope to say.

"We've already spent half a lifetime together, Lilac Sophia. How does forever sound to you?"

On the stage in front of us, our class's valedictorian has finished her speech. The crowd erupts in applause.

It's our graduation day. I'm not there.

Chapter Twenty-Four

Allison's wedding falls exactly three weeks before my sixteenth birthday. She wanted a winter wedding, she said, with poinsettias and Christmas trees and snow blanketing the ground. But it sucks for her because the pine needles are already falling off the trees and instead of snow, the yard in front of the church is like one big swampland, thanks to the never-ending rain of the past week.

Like I said. Unraveling.

We're sitting around the kitchen table stuffing Jordan almonds into white organza favor bags and listening to Mom and Dad bicker about who's going to bring me and my wheelchair from here to the church and from the church to the reception.

"I can drive her to the church," Kurt says with a smile for me. Allison melts at his chivalry. Whether from the medicine coursing through my veins or the disgusting display of sweetness before me, I'm fighting the urge to gag.

"You," my mother says to him, grabbing a handful of candy, "are going to be too busy with your groomsmen."

I snicker at the subtext, which earns me a glare from both of my parents and my sister. I pop a Jordan almond in my mouth, nausea-be-damned.

It's not that I don't like Kurt. He's been dating my sister since their freshman year of college, so it really was only a matter of time before they got engaged. It's just that he's so…*nice*. And the last thing we need is someone nice and normal like him coming in and making us realize how messed up our family actually is.

No one wants to look in the mirror someone else is holding up.

"She's right," my dad says, and the fact that he's agreeing with my mom takes even him by surprise. "You'll have plenty else to take care of on your big day. We'll get Lilac there."

Do they have to? I mean, really… They've hired a professional videographer for this thing—can't they just send me a clip reel of the important parts?

"What about Rebecca?" My mom still can't say the name without her mouth twisting up at the corners, like she just took a bite out of a sour lemon. To Dad's credit, he wasn't the one to bring his fiancée into this conversation. But then again, he is the one who ended their marriage.

"Maybe the Emerys can take her," Allison offers.

My head shoots up at this, and I stare at each of them across the table. "No."

"Why not?" she asks. "Nathan just got his license, didn't he?"

"No." I shake my head so hard, I'm a little afraid I'll get whiplash. "No way in hell."

"I'm sure he won't mind."

"Did you hear me? I said no…"

"We can stick the wheelchair in the back of his truck."

"I'll tell you where else we can stick it—"

"Oh, will you grow up, Lilac!"

My mom gasps and covers her mouth. Dad and Kurt exchange glances. Allison pales, realizing what she's said a second too late, but I already feel the slap of her words. I pull my sleeve up and wave my arm, dangling the few inches of tubing protruding from my underarm before the PICC line disappears beneath my skin.

"I'm trying, Allison!" I yell as I back away from the table and wheel myself into the living room. "Believe me, I'm trying to grow up."

Fifteen's almost over. Maybe sixteen will be better.

SUMMER

Chapter Twenty-Five

LILAC

16 YEARS, 6 MONTHS

Dr. Wilhems doesn't make house calls, which is a shame because I liked him. Now it's my mother and the new home nurse fussing over me like I'm a toddler. Maybe I am. Maybe I'm two years old today and that's why they keep popping their head into my room to see if I'm still breathing.

I'm still here. I'm still breathing.

If I'm two today, it'll be years before I stop.

Chapter Twenty-Six

We decide to go away for summer vacation our senior year of college. In a few short months, we'll be spread across the world—my best friend, Kate, moving to Boston for grad school; my boyfriend, Dan, heading to New York for publishing; and me—following one of them until I figure out what I want to do with my life. We resolve that life can't be only death and college loans and so, one night before the end of the semester, when we're drunk on Southern Comfort and lounging in Dan's apartment, we plan to rent a house on the California coast as one last hurrah before the conformity of adulthood.

Up until now, it's the farthest I've been away from home, but when I'm thirty-one I'll taste wine at the vineyards in Tuscany, and when I'm forty-four, I'll watch artists draw caricatures for tourists in Montmartre, and when I'm fifty, I'll shop at open-air markets in Ankara.

But today, I'm twenty-one and lounging on a beach chair, hot sand collecting between my toes. Beside me, Kate is rummaging through the cooler for the drinks we've packed. In front of me is the ocean—and Dan and Nathan.

Nathan. Why, oh why is Nathan here? Good question. It just so happens that he's Dan's best friend, which doesn't bode well for my wish to never see him except for when we're both home over Thanksgiving and winter breaks. He's always in our apartment—and not just when Dan is around. I have a feeling he has a crush on Kate, and I can't say I blame him. She's blonde and athletic and has this effervescent personality that somehow never seems to rub off on me.

She's what I wish I could be. At least, she's what I wish people would see in me.

"Beer?" she asks, holding out a bottle.

I shake my head. She calls to the guys, and I watch them crowd around her lounge chair. Dan is trying to wipe stray grains of sand off her towel for her, and Nathan is smiling at something she said. I don't know why, but suddenly the air feels too hot and the beach feels too crowded, and I wonder how it is I'm still here breathing.

I stumble to my feet, blinking back hot tears, and quickly pull on my cover up.

"You know, I think I forgot my sunscreen."

Kate glances up, then reaches into her bag. "Here, you can use mine."

"Nope, that's okay," I say, busying myself with my sandals, trying to avoid looking at them. I can feel Nathan's eyes on me, but I don't want to hear whatever it is he has to say. I wish he wasn't on this trip, wish it was just me and Dan so we can get back to that cocoon we've created for ourselves the last two months, where I was the one he looked at like that. I want to be the one someone looks at like that.

"I'm going to run back to the house." I pause. "Dan, you can, uh, join me, if you want."

He raises an eyebrow, his lips spreading into a slow smile. He doesn't expect that of me. Of course not—Kate's the kind of girl with all the sex appeal, not me. I don't know what I was thinking. I feel stupid for even trying. I'm gone before he can say anything.

The ocean is roaring to life behind me, and I pass sunbathers and a volleyball game as I trudge up the sand dune towards the house. The farther away I get from them, the easier I can breathe, and I take a few steady breaths and hastily wipe my eyes, scolding myself for feeling jealous of my best friend, for not feeling like enough of me.

Back at the house, the air-conditioning is a blessing, and I pause in the doorway and let the cold air wash over me, relishing and cursing the silence of the house all at once. This silence means I can think, but I don't know if I want to be alone with my thoughts.

My suntan lotion is in the bottom of my toiletries bag on the bathroom sink, but I don't intend to get it. Instead, I grab a glass from the drainboard and run the tap. There are nautilus shells lining the windowsill, circular shapes in varying patterns, and I admire them for a moment, if only to avoid looking down to the beach where I know I'll see my friends laughing and enjoying the sun—with me or without me. I take a long sip of water and finally skim the crowd. Sure enough, there's Dan, sitting closer to Kate than he was before, leaning in to say something before she throws her head back to laugh and playfully push him away.

"He's not coming."

I don't jump at his voice. In fact, I almost expect it. He's standing at the patio door, and I walk past him and sink to the couch, deflated. He closes the screen behind him and leans against the counter like he's waiting for something, waiting for me.

"What do you want, Nathan?" I ask. "Why are you here?"

He shrugs. "I didn't want to see you get hurt."

"And you?"

"What about me?"

"You're not hurt?"

"What—because of Kate?" There's actual surprise in his voice, and I'm taken aback. "Jesus, Lilac, I thought you'd get it by now. You're so smart, but you're so—"

"I'm so what?" I challenge him. "Go on."

He doesn't take the bait. He's calm, looking me squarely in the eyes. "You drive me crazy sometimes."

It's not the way he says it—because if anything, he sounds exasperated—but it's those words he chooses. I've heard them before, and I'll hear them again. I cross the room to stand beside him, looking out the window at Kate and Dan now walking along the shoreline. Nathan is facing the living room, his arms crossed, shoulders tense like he's afraid to move a muscle. We stand in that silence, something unsaid growing between us. I look past the surfers in the waves, near where the sun is beginning to dip along the horizon.

"Why are you here?" I ask again, my voice quiet. I'm holding my breath, afraid to hear the answer, desperately waiting for it. Beside me, I can feel him turn, feel those eyes on me again. When he speaks, his voice is low and tender.

"Because," he says, and the silence is so prolonged, I raise my eyes to look at him. "Because you drive me crazy."

I decide I like being twenty-one.

Chapter Twenty-Seven

LILAC

16 YEARS, 6 MONTHS

I watched a *National Geographic* special about the nautilus once. They're cephalopods, like the octopus and squid, and live deep in the ocean with shells that are shaped like a spiral. On the outside, the shells aren't much to look at, but the inside contains a pearl veneer and is split into different chambers. The older the nautilus gets and the more it outgrows its shell, the more chambers form along the spiral, and with each season, the nautilus moves into a bigger and better chamber. According to studies, they can live well past twenty years this way.

Lucky bastards.

Chapter Twenty-Eight

NATHAN

"Heard dinner was a disaster."

I snort and press a button on the remote in my hand. "You should have been there."

"Glad I wasn't." A pause. "So, you really haven't talked to them since?"

"Two months."

"Nate—"

I groan and turn off the TV, throwing my arm over the back of the couch as I whirl around to meet Jamie's stare. "I have this conversation with Jess every morning. I can't have it with you, too. That's not why I'm here."

My sister's expression softens. She puts down the spatula, turns the burner on the stovetop to low, and crosses the kitchen into the living room where she sits on the edge of the coffee table. I sigh and slump further into the couch cushions.

"*Please…*" I groan and throw my head back, begging her not to turn this into one of her therapy sessions, but she goes right for the jugular anyway, bypassing any pretenses.

"Why did you come here?"

Because I've been having this conversation with Jess every morning, I want to say to her. And I really don't want to have it again.

For the past two weeks, I've been hightailing it out of Jess's house before breakfast and heading over to Jamie's. Jamie's never there—already headed to the library to get in a couple of hours of work on her dissertation. The first time I knocked on the door, her girlfriend opened it, immediately asked if I was okay, then told me to make myself at home while she went back to bed without further questioning. After a week, she handed me a key. Today, Jamie was waiting in the living room, arms crossed and a frown on her face.

Fuck.

She didn't say anything. Just raised her eyebrows, pointed to the couch, and wandered into the kitchen to rifle through the fridge.

Despite being fifteen months apart and looking like twins for most of their life—same curly hair, same high cheekbones, same curl of the lip when they smile—my sisters couldn't be more different, and looking around the apartment, that's never been more apparent. Jamie's place looks like her room did when she was still living back home—mandalas and wire sculptures, paper lanterns and patchwork blankets. Everything in bold colors because that's Jamie. Bold.

When she was thirteen, she dyed her hair bright red, nearly giving my mother a heart attack. It's been some variation of that same color ever since. At sixteen, she got her nose pierced. Mom grounded her, and Dad—well, he didn't notice until later and by then, it was out of his jurisdiction to say anything. She got her first tattoo as soon as she turned eighteen—a black and white owl on the back of her upper arm. I asked her what it meant, and she just smiled and said something along the lines of, "Perspective is everything, little brother." My mom once caught her burning sage in her room. She mostly left Jamie alone after that. I think she was just relieved to know it wasn't pot.

I like Jamie. I know you're supposed to love your family and all—and maybe I do, as fucked up as we are—but I actually like my sister. She lets me be me—no questions, no assumptions, no expectations. Half the time, I don't even have to talk for her to know what I'm feeling, and that means something. And even then, she leaves me alone, and that matters, too.

Which is why it's her apartment I immediately head to in the mornings when I need to escape Jess's interrogations and Tim's lectures on forgiveness and forget about everything for a while. Because here, among her incense sticks and Buddha statues, I forget everything for a while. At least here it feels like some kind of refuge—a temporary respite where I can pretend, for those few hours, that I'm actually someplace called home.

I should know better.

"You know you're always welcome here, baby brother. But it's not going to do you any good to keep holding onto the pain of the past."

Coming from Jamie, those words—those same words that both Jess and Tim used just this morning—don't seem so infuriating. I bow my head, listening to her talk about how forgiving someone isn't about them at all, and suddenly she's there—

Lilac.

Lilac at six, wearing overalls and purple sneakers. Lilac at eleven, bundled in a sunshine-yellow jacket as we study the stars. Lilac this past Christmas, wearing a maroon bridesmaid's dress and a scowl on her face that made me grin and my heart lurch when she opened the door.

Lilac, my best friend. The only person who made it feel like I was always home, when I never had a real home to go to. Could she ever forgive me? Would she?

I want to see her, but the thought creates a weight in my stomach. What if she doesn't want to talk to me? After everything between us, after all this time, what if she doesn't care if our friendship is repaired? And even if she did want that, would it be enough?

Would there still be time?

"You have to reconcile sometime, Nate."

I lift my head. For a split second, I think Jamie's talking about Lilac, too. But then she raises an eyebrow, and I exhale heavily. "Like you did?"

"My situation is different," Jamie says, standing up and wandering back into the kitchen. "I never had a relationship with Dad."

"Lucky you."

"But that doesn't mean I didn't want one." I watch Jamie scrape the scrambled eggs onto a plate, then grab a fork from the drawer. "Sometimes people are worth a second chance. It's up to you to figure out who those people are." She holds the plate out to me. "Promise me you'll at least think about it."

I promise her. But it's not my dad I'm thinking about.

Chapter Twenty-Nine

LILAC

16 YEARS, 7 MONTHS

Dr. Wilhems knocks on my door and pokes his head in, holding his hand up in a wave.

"Didn't want to wake you if you were asleep," he says. I blink my eyes a few times, trying to ease the fog from my mind, and struggle to sit up. "No, no, don't get up," he says, but he's at my side in a second, adjusting the pillows behind my back.

"I thought doctors didn't make house calls." My throat is hoarse, and I lick my chapped lips, then glance at the glass of water on my bedside table. I don't have the energy to reach for it.

Today I'm eighty-nine.

He follows my gaze and walks to the other side of the bed to retrieve it, holding the straw up to my parched lips while I suck in the water greedily, then cough because it's too much, too fast. The coughing leads to a wave of dizziness, and my head falls back against the pillows. I squeeze my eyes shut tight.

"Easy, easy," he soothes. His fingers are light on my wrist as he suspends it in air, his eyes focused on his watch. After a minute, he pats the back of my hand and rests it on the bed. "If I knew I was gonna have that kind of a reception, I'd have come sooner."

"You here to check up on me?"

"Just for a visit," he says. "But since I'm here..."

He spends a few minutes at the IV monitor, checks my PICC lines. My eyes flutter closed, and I'm just about to drift off when I hear him speak again.

"Mind if I sit?"

"As long as you don't mind if I fall asleep mid-sentence."

"Tell you what," he says, dragging the chair closer to the bed. "Soon as you get tired of me, you can kick me out."

I don't remind him that all I ever am anymore is tired. I don't tell him that's what you get for being eighty-nine.

"My mom?"

"Downstairs with your nurse."

"That bad, huh? They had to bring in the big guns?"

He smiles at this. I still like his smile. He looks like my grandpa, reminds me of my dad—at least, who I wish my dad could have been. Dr. Wilhems doesn't seem like the kind of dad who would leave his family when things got tough. Especially not since he's the one sitting here now while my dad is off on his honeymoon with his second wife because "You have to live life when you have the chance, honey."

Fuck him. Fuck him for living his life when I still have the chance. I still have a chance...

"Nothing like that," Dr. Wilhems says, and he shifts in the chair, opens and closes his mouth like he doesn't know how he wants to start. "I gotta tell you a secret about us doctors, Lila. We have our favorite patients." I raise my eyebrows. "I know, I know..." He chuckles. "But sometimes we can't compartmentalize. Sometimes a patient sneaks in there, leaving a footprint on our lives."

I watch him struggle to find his words, searching my face for any sign of understanding. I know exactly where he's heading with this.

"The ones you can't save."

It's not a question, but he nods slowly. "More than the ones we can." He clears his throat. "I'm doing everything I can, sweetheart. There's a new treatment coming out of Germany…"

I shake my head, turn away. I'm weak. I'm tired.

I'm eighty-nine years old.

Chapter Thirty

Somehow over the course of the night, we ended up here, in the backyard of an old Victorian house that's been divided into apartments for college kids, sitting on picnic benches around a campfire while a handful of kids play beer pong on the other side of the yard. There's a buffet on the patio—empty pizza boxes and stray chip crumbs and soda cans sitting next to a tapped-out keg—and we're all wearing those cheap plastic leis you can buy in bulk. The party has petered out to a small group of us chatting around the fire, listening to some of the music majors strum their guitars in harmony.

Nathan's sitting across the fire from me. When he looks up from his conversation, I can see the firelight dance in his eyes. I haven't talked to him since I got here. I don't know what I would say to him even if I had the chance. We didn't expect to be attending the same school, and now here we are, four weeks into our first semester and at the same party.

Someone's passing around jello shots, and Kate tosses her empty cup on the ground and reaches for the tray.

"Whoa," the guy next to her says, passing the tray above her head. "I think you've had enough."

"Fuck you, Dan." She reaches for the tray again, tumbles over the bench.

"No, fuck the fact that you stole my byline for the McCrary Hall protest. Why the hell are you even at this party, Kate?"

I don't want to be involved in this. Seriously, this is the last thing I want to be involved in. I glance across the fire to Nathan, and though he's keeping his head down, I can tell he's listening. I can't tell what he's thinking.

"Okay, well, you can fuck off then," Dan is saying. I watch Kate storm off, and I sigh and mutter goodbye before walking after her, dumping the lei in the trash on my way out.

"I hate this piece of shit town!" Kate sings, bitterness in her voice and arms spread wide as we walk up the block towards the dorms. I'm several steps behind her—I don't even know if she knows I'm here—but I keep my distance and let her yell, earning us glares and a few giggles from couples on their way to their own parties. "I don't even know why I came here. It's not like a four-point-oh from a state school is going to impress the admissions people at Boston College or NYU or wherever the hell I go to grad school. Oh, God." She freezes, her hand flying up to her mouth. For a second I think she's going to hurl, and I pray she does it in the bushes and not right there on the sidewalk. But she whirls around, her eyes wide. "I didn't even think of that. What if I don't get into grad school, Lila? What if I don't get in anywhere?"

Her hair has come loose from her ponytail and spreads across her shoulders, wild and free. I wish I had a mirror because I want to show her that's who she is—someone who has always been wild and free, and no school should ever tie her down. But it's not what she wants to hear. So I tell her those schools would be crazy not to take her and that she's only a freshman now and needs to quit putting so much pressure on herself.

"Easy for you to say," she scoffs. "Your parents don't give a shit what you do."

It's only half the truth. My parents would care too much, if they could. They'd wonder after my grades and scold me for drinking too much at backyard parties and then say I was a good girl for making sure my drunk best friend got home safely but to never do it again. They'd drive me up to school and help me unpack my new comforter and books and floor lamp, and then they'd take me out to lunch in the dining hall to try out the food before hugging me goodbye with tears in their eyes and traveling back home—together.

I wish that were the case. I wish I could have that college experience. I wish so many things.

But now they don't care because my story goes a little bit different than that...

I can't think about that, though. Because tonight I'm eighteen and my best friend needs me, and it feels good to be needed instead of the other way around.

"Come on," I say, throwing an arm around her shoulders as we wander through the lobby of our dorm. "Everything always feels better in the morning." I pause. "Except you— you're probably going to feel like shit."

Her roommate is already asleep by the time we stumble into her room, waking up only when Kate vomits into the tiny wastebasket by her desk. Her roommate glares and climbs down from the top bunk and pulls a bottle of water out of the mini-fridge.

"This is the last time, Lila, I swear," she warns, and I thank her and leave her to put Kate to bed.

It's so late that by the time I'm heading upstairs to my own dorm room, the campus has quieted— the only sounds are from muffled televisions behind closed doors. I fling open the stairwell door and turn down my hallway and freeze.

Nathan's sitting on the floor next to my door, legs outstretched and hands stuffed in the pockets of his jacket. He looks up as I approach, and I open my mouth to speak, but I'm cut off when my neighbor walks out of her room across the hall. She glances at the two of us, tugs on the ties of her terrycloth robe to make sure it's secure, then scampers down the hallway. We watch her disappear into the bathroom.

"What are you doing here?" I ask as Nathan scrambles to his feet.

"Did Kate get back okay?"

"Yeah, her roommate's taking care of her." He nods, and I wait for him to say something more, but he's silent and stoic, and I don't like that combination. The small spark of hope that maybe he came to see me—*me*—begins to grow dim, and I pull my keys out of my coat pocket and step towards the door. "Okay, well, goodnight."

"Wait, Lilac—" He holds his hand out to stop me, his fingers brushing my arm—light to the touch, but it burns me all the way through. "Will you come outside with me?"

I snort. "No."

"Just for a few minutes, just for a walk."

"Now? It's, like, three in the morning."

He runs a hand through his hair in frustration. "Do you always have to be so difficult?"

"Yes. It's part of my charm."

"You really want to call it that?"

I glare at him. There's the Nathan Emery I've known since I was six. "That's not exactly the way to get in my good graces, you know."

He sighs, but his eyes soften. I can't remember the last time I saw him look so serious.

"Please."

Or heard him beg.

"Five minutes," I say. "Then I'm going to bed. *Alone.*"

He smirks but doesn't say anything. I want to punch him, but I'm eighteen today. Not twelve-going-on-thirteen.

I follow him outside and across the wide expanse of lawn, down past the parking lot and over the train tracks, to a small playground sitting on the outskirts of a schoolyard.

"The swings? Really?" I shove my hands in the pockets of my jacket. "Nate, it's three AM and I'm tired. What are we doing here?"

He slows to a stop and turns around. Beneath the lamplight I can see the smirk is gone from his lips, replaced with something I can't yet name. "You haven't called me that since we were kids."

"We haven't been to a playground since we were kids."

Rust has begun to set in on the equipment, making the chains squeak as he folds himself onto the swing. I don't know how to judge what's happening here, so I sit at the bottom of the metal slide and watch Nathan sway back and forth, waiting for him to speak.

"Remember how we used to see who could fly the highest?" he finally asks, a smile in his voice.

"You mean the time I broke my arm because you convinced me I could fly at all?"

His lips spread into a grin. "Yeah, that's the one."

That really happened. My mother was livid and wouldn't let me play with Nathan for the rest of the summer, but I think it was meant more as a punishment for me than for him. She made me wear a helmet and knee pads even when I was roller-skating in the driveway, and when Gretchen Kelly from a few blocks away invited me to a sleepover, she insisted on driving me instead of letting me ride my bike.

My cast was supposed to come off a few days after the start of third grade, so everyone in my class was able to sign it with colored markers. Everyone except Nathan. He sat across the aisle from me on the bus the second day of school, and when the bus turned into our neighborhood, he finally got up the nerve to ask if there was a spot for him. I showed him a blank space near my wrist. I didn't tell him I'd been saving it for him. He wrote two words, his block handwriting large and slanted, then pulled something out of his pocket and pressed it against my cast. He was down the bus steps before I could figure out what it was—a sticker of a bird, wings outstretched.

"Hey, Lilac!" he yelled across the yard. "Told ya you could fly."

The memory makes me uncomfortable. So much has happened between us since then. So much has changed. I lean back into the curve of the slide and stare up at the sky. Wisps of clouds pass in front of the moon, blocking out the light for minutes at a time. The stars seem vast and closer than they've ever been. I want to believe I've never seen stars like this. I want to be captivated by their bright clusters and wonder how I could have spent my whole life beneath this sky and never have bothered to look up, but that's another lie. I've seen these stars before.

"What happened to us, Lilac?"

Nathan's voice sounds faraway, even though he's right nearby. I pull my gaze from the stars and sit up, shaking my head because, no. We're not doing this here, not now. Not when we've had all summer—hell, all these years—to figure it out.

"What?" He seems surprised by my anger, even more surprised when I jump to my feet and begin to walk away. "What—Lilac…"

"Are you kidding me right now?" I whirl around. "Nathan, it's *three* in the *morning*."

"I know, I know!" He grits his teeth in frustration, runs a hand along the back of his head. "I just needed to talk to someone—"

"And I was the only someone that came to mind." I throw my hands in the air. "Got it. Great. I'm going home."

He's on his feet in an instant, reaching for my hand. Even when I stop, he doesn't let go. "It's not like that, Lilac. It's never been like that with you. Don't you get that by now?" His eyes are searching mine for any understanding, but I don't know if I have any to give. I don't know what he wants. "You—"

He cuts himself off, drops my hand and wanders over to the merry-go-round. I'm aware of how empty and cold my hand feels now without him holding it, aware of the space between us, and I'm so surprised at how hollow I feel without him standing next to me that I thrust both hands in my coat pockets like that will get them warm.

"My dad moved out." His voice is so quiet, I have to step forward to make sure I heard him right.

"They're separating?"

"Nope," he says. "Skipping right past that step and going straight for the divorce."

I bite my lip, then bridge the rest of the distance between us and sit down beside him, only a metal bar separating us. He's pushing around stray wood chips in the dirt with his foot, the rhythm making the merry-go-round sway back and forth.

"Has he—"

"Stopped drinking?" Nathan scoffs. "If there's one thing that man loves more than himself, it's his alcohol."

Nathan wasn't drinking at the party tonight. He didn't toast at my sister's wedding. I can't believe I forgot that. I think back on all the times I imagined him—imagined us—and I wonder how I could have gotten it so wrong.

"I just don't know what to do about my mom, you know? How am I supposed to leave her alone and go about my life?"

"She wants you to live your life, you know that."

"Come on, Lilac." He shakes his head. "That's bullshit. That's what everyone says, but there's still some secret part of them that hopes you'll press pause and take care of them."

He's not wrong. I think about my sister out in Phoenix and how she can only seem to talk about crown moulding and cabinet hardware when she calls, think about my dad and the postcards from his honeymoon I immediately toss in the trash. Sometimes, you want to be a little selfish. Sometimes, you don't want life to go on for everyone else— at least, not yet. Not while you're still hurting.

"You're right," I say.

He turns to look at me, his hair falling into his eyes again, and I fight the urge to reach up and brush it away. "How was it when your parents got divorced?"

"Well, they have a kid who's dying and only one parent who knows how to handle that, so… A little different."

I didn't say that. I wish I had said that, wish we sat there on that merry-go-round in the middle of our first semester of college, baring our souls under a three AM sky, but it never happened.

I haven't talked to Nathan since my sister's wedding.

Chapter Thirty-One

My sister's wedding. You know how they say reality is sometimes weirder than your dreams? That's my sister's wedding. I promise, this one's all true.

Allison marries her long-time boyfriend, Kurt, the week before Christmas in the church in the neighboring development—the same church where Mom insisted I attend Sunday school for years and then promptly stopped attending mass herself once she figured out my dad was screwing his sales associate.

Oh, you thought I meant his accountant?

Yeah. She came later.

When I think about it, we all had a pretty good reason to be pissed at God, and what better way to say suck it than to ditch his weekly party. Turns out, though, that's not at all how it's supposed to work, and Mom's been trying to repent for that particular sin ever since.

As for me? I've spent enough time indoors to know you can't find faith within four walls. Just like I know prayers don't work the way we want them to and hardly as we expect them to. The devil in my body taught me that.

It's not that I don't believe in God. It's just that I don't think this whole life and death thing works the way we think it does. If I thought this was the absolute end, that would be one thing, but I can't believe we only get one shot at this—with all our flaws and fuck ups. Life can't be that merciless, to have to spend these years staring down death only to be greeted by eternal oblivion. I have to believe there's something else, something more—have to find reason in this abject rhyme—because that's the only way I can be okay with this. And I have to be okay with this. I don't have a choice.

Anyway. If I actually believed God was a punishing god and wanted to demand penance for not attending church, I'd say he did a pretty good job—and with a sense of humor to boot—the day of Allison's wedding.

It's a flurry of activity in our household, which I happily watch from my place on the couch while I administer my own infusion. The sky outside is overcast, and I'm keeping a close eye on the storm clouds that seem to be gathering strength. I have ten bucks on a bet with my dad that it will rain.

"I don't know," Kurt had said at the rehearsal dinner the night before. "They say rain's good luck on your wedding day."

"Not if you're in a Guns N' Roses video."

"Jesus, Lilac!" My sister dropped her fork, anxiety etched across her face. "You can't say those things!"

"Really, Lilac," Mom admonished.

Dad winked at me. "Five bucks?"

I shook my head. If I was gonna win this thing, I wanted him to pay. "Let's make it ten."

Now it really does seem like it's going to storm, and my sister is, as expected, freaking out.

"Let's get to the church," my mom is saying, her voice calm and placating as she ushers my sister out the door. "We can check on the flowers and figure out what to do about pictures."

My dad, arms full with my sister's wedding dress and make-up bag, pauses and looks at me sprawled on the couch. "You're, um… You're sure you're fine with all this?"

I can't tell if he means the wedding or pumping myself full of medicine, so I just nod and say, "I'm fine, Dad. I'll see you at the church."

I see him glance towards the alcohol swabs and packages of flush syringes spread out on the coffee table, then at the piece of tube sock that covers the PICC line in my arm, but he quickly averts his eyes when he catches me looking. I want to comfort him—tell him it's not that bad, it doesn't hurt, that I've already done this dozens of times before on my own—but I don't. He doesn't deserve it.

"Don't forget, Mr. and Mrs. Emery will be coming for you at one."

Then, he's gone.

I get dressed in my bridesmaid's dress—a cranberry-colored chiffon gown with a matching wrap that'll hide my line—and apply some eyeshadow and lip gloss and wait on the couch for the Emerys, closing my eyes because it's barely the afternoon and already I can feel myself growing tired.

Finally, the doorbell rings at a quarter to one. When I open it, Nathan's standing there in a pair of dress pants, a sage green button-down shirt, and a smirk I want to slap off his face.

"Lilac Sophia."

"I hate you."

He laughs. "All I said was your name."

"Yeah, well, that's enough. Where are your parents?" I glance out the door behind him, but only Nathan's truck is sitting in their driveway.

"Dad, um…" He clears his throat, shifts uneasily. "Dad forgot to pick up the gift like Mom asked him to. They left a little while ago, said I was supposed to give you a lift." His face brightens again, and I sigh and grab my bag and coat and point to the wheelchair.

"You need to give that a lift," I say.

"Aren't you supposed to, you know, be sitting in it?"

"Only when I need to. And I don't need to."

Actually, I do. Today's a bad day, made worse by the impending rainstorm. I can already feel my skin growing clammy, and my legs are more like weights, but I don't want to give him the satisfaction. He shrugs and wheels the chair down the front steps, and I shut the door and follow after him.

In the truck, he sees me shivering, wrapping my coat closer around my body, and he turns the heat up, keeps the vents turned on me.

"Better?"

I nod and keep my gaze focused on the glovebox in front of me, trying to ignore the houses rushing past as we turn out of the neighborhood and pick up speed on the main road.

"If you hurl, can you make sure you do it out the window?"

I hate him. I hate him. I hate him.

He keeps glancing over at me, his face full of concern, until I glare at him and promise if I do vomit, it'll be all over him.

At the church, a small crowd of guests have begun to filter up the steps before disappearing through the double doors. My dad's waiting for us in the doorway, and Nathan pulls up to the curb before helping him maneuver the wheelchair out of the cargo bed. My dad offers me his arm, and I hold onto him and grip the stair railing as I slowly ascend the steps. Nathan passes us on his way back to his truck.

"Hey, Lilac," he says when he reaches the sidewalk. I turn around. "You really do look beautiful."

Then he hops in his truck and drives away to park.

My dad raises an eyebrow. "You got something going on with the Emery kid?"

"Nope."

But I can't stop the blush from creeping into my cheeks or the fact that my stomach is doing all sorts of flips, and not just from the medicine coursing into my already-racing heart.

Chapter Thirty-Two

He takes my hand.

"Where are we going?" I ask, trying to ignore the warmth that's flooding through my body at his touch. I feel like I'm a teenager again, strolling towards the sunset with the boy who occupies every corner of my heart. Except he's not a boy anymore. And I'm not a teenager.

"You'll see," he says with a grin. He tugs me closer, puts his arm around me, and I lean into him and inhale.

The sun has just begun to set on the horizon, painting the sky in shades of gold. In the neighborhood around us, moms are pulling into driveways in minivans and dads are standing at the front door, calling out to kids playing in the yard that dinner's ready and to get inside and wash up if they know what's good for them. I don't know these neighbors. I should because I grew up here, but I'm not a child anymore, either. So much has changed.

We follow a path past a small grove of trees and approach the back end of a park. He grins and tugs me along past the baseball diamond, past the basketball court and pavilions, to the playground that's since been abandoned for dinnertime.

"Seriously?" I ask with a laugh. "Nathan, what are we doing here?"

This is not how I expect our first date to go.

Nathan grins and lets go of my hand, hoisting himself over the playset's guardrail and landing on the wooden bridge with a thud. The bridge shakes, its planks rattling together to create a hollow echo in the air. He laughs and jumps again, and I can't help but think here's the boy I knew when I was young—this goofy, charming boy who always seemed ready for a laugh but whose smile always seemed to hide something deeper, something somber, a Nathan I could never fully reach. Now the sorrow has disappeared so it's just him with a bright smile and laughter in his eyes, asking me to join him and leave the world behind.

Asking me to remember how to be a kid again with him.

I duck around him and hop onto the landing of the playground, holding out a hand to stop him from following me. "Nope." I stretch out my arms like I'm claiming the space. "I'm the queen of this castle, and this is my dominion!"

Nathan takes a step back, eyebrows arched in amusement. "Oh, yeah?" He crosses his arms. "Is that so."

"It is."

"So, what would that make me?"

I try to stifle a giggle, my eyes locked on his. "My fool."

His eyes light up, his grin grows wider. Before I can say another word, his hands are sliding around my waist, lifting me off the step and whirling me around, placing me firmly in the mulch.

"Hey!"

Nathan laughs and climbs the steps to the top level of the playground. "The queen has been dethroned."

"Treachery!" I gasp.

"Flattery will get you nowhere." He winks and disappears through the covered slide.

I run up the steps after him, follow him back down. He's waiting for me at the bottom of the slide, hands placed on either side of the ledge, blocking me from getting up. There's something in his eyes, something in the way he's staring at me that makes me lean back; he leans closer. My breath hitches.

"You've stolen the castle," I say quietly.

"You've stolen so much more than that, Lilac Sophia."

He backs up suddenly, the seriousness gone from his eyes, his lips lifting in that familiar grin. "Race you to the swings!"

We play. We chase each other down the slide and across the monkey bars and through the castle turrets. We climb the wall made of colored tires and push each other on the swings and spin around and around on the merry-go-round until we grow dizzy with delight.

"I needed that," I say, breathless from laughter. We're laying on our backs on the inner circle of the merry-go-round, barely touching except for our hands entwined above our heads. Occasionally, he'll stroke the back of my hand with his thumb, as if making sure I'm real, that I'm still there in the moment with him. "How did you know I needed that?"

He turns his head to look at me and grins, but he doesn't answer.

"God, I haven't played like that since... I don't even know when." I pause and stare at the sky, purple now with the darkening night. A scattering of stars peeks out beneath the velvet blanket, constellations shifting as we rotate on our own axis. "Why do you think it took us this long?"

Confusion flits across his face. "What, to come here?"

"No, I mean us," I clarify. "Like this. To find each other."

"We were never lost, Lilac," he says. He slips his hand from mine and runs his fingers across my forehead, smoothing back my hair. "We just took the long way around."

We're thirty years old today. We've known each other since we were six.

Maybe some people really are worth waiting for.

He slips his arm beneath me, and I snuggle closer to him, rest a hand on his chest. We're comfortable in this silence together, each of us lost in thought and the nearness of each other. That's what happens when you've been together practically your whole life. Sometimes words don't need to be said.

"Do you believe there's life up there?" he asks finally.

It's late—eight, maybe nine o'clock. It's hard to tell. We've lost track of the time. The stars have multiplied, sprinkling the blanket of darkened sky until we feel like we're lost ourselves.

I sit up so I can look at him. "Do you?"

"After all these years, looking at a sky like that? I have to believe in something."

I inhale, soak up his words, let them move through me. I don't tell him how often I've been questioning my beliefs lately, wondering what comes next. Wondering if there's anything at all. I don't tell him there's still some part of me that feels the same as when I was young, believing in uncharted worlds and infinite lifetimes. I don't know what to do with my conflicting theories. It feels too simple and so complicated all at once, and there's a part of me that just wants to chalk everything about this universe up to one big, cosmic joke.

"What about life after… You know." I let my voice trail off and turn my head to look at him, but he's already staring at me. "What do you think about that?"

"I look at you," he repeats himself, "at us, and I have to believe in something."

He leans forward. I close my eyes. Our lips meet.

It's not our first kiss. Not even close.

Chapter Thirty-Three

SEVEN MONTHS EARLIER

My mom walks me down the aisle because I'm too weak to make it on my own, and I'll be damned if I'm rolling myself in a wheelchair with a hundred pairs of eyes on me. To anyone who doesn't know my body is trying to kill me, I'm sure it looks like a sweet moment of family bonding, and how lovely it was for Allison to want everyone to play a part in her ceremony. To my mother, who is squeezing my hand a little too tight, I'm sure it's a reminder that this might be the first and last time she'll be a Mother of the Bride.

I force myself not to look at her. I don't think I'll be able to get through this if I do.

I'm supposed to be a bridesmaid—up there with Allison's friends from college who are named Jasmine and Belle and Ariel like this is some farcical parade of Disney princesses—but there's a seat with my name on it between my parents in the first row of pews. In a few minutes, my dad will join us and sit on the other side of me, but now I'm acting as a buffer between my mom and Rebecca. Every so often, Rebecca will glance up from her program and smile nervously at one of us, but when she catches my mother's eye, she'll find the names of the wedding party just as fascinating as I do.

"Where's Mulan?" I whisper to my mom.

"What?"

"Mulan. Or Pocahontas. They're missing the show."

"For the love of God, Lilac, I cannot handle your nonsense today."

Lilac. I bet I would have made a great Disney princess if I were strong enough to stand up there with them.

The music changes, and the congregation rises and turns towards the door. My mom helps me to my feet, and on the other side, I can feel someone's light touch on my back to help steady me. When I glance over my shoulder, Rebecca pulls her hand away quickly, like maybe she's overstepped, but I smile and whisper thanks. She's not the one I blame.

My sister's making her way down the aisle. Everyone is angled towards her, turned away from us. Everyone but one. Nathan is sitting a few rows back, but it's hard to miss him, even in the crowd. While everyone else is watching the bride, he's watching me.

Chapter Thirty-Four

"Do you, Lilac Sophia Carpenter, take this man, Nathaniel Oliver Emery—"

"Oliver? Sorry, hold on. Your middle name's Oliver?"

"Actually, it's not, and you know it's not."

"Right. My mind's kind of fuzzy today. I can't remember."

"You know everything about me and you can't remember my middle name?"

"Well, when you put it like that, I've got a new name for you…"

"I hate to interrupt, but may we continue?"

"Sorry, Father."

"Yes, sorry, Father."

"As we were. Lilac, do you take Nathan…"

I wish, I wish, I wish…

Chapter Thirty-Five

It takes my Aunt Mildred—yes, I have an Aunt Mildred—exactly four minutes at the end of cocktail hour to corner me and ask how I'm holding up. And considering I'm in my wheelchair at this point, I'm not holding up very well at all.

I don't actually have an Aunt Mildred. At least, that's not her real name. Her name is Margaret, and she's my grandmother's last surviving sister which, at eighty years old, seems like she landed in the better end of the gene pool. We call her Mildred because my mother didn't know she existed for the first thirty years of her life, and then once they actually met, she only wished she didn't. Margaret was, apparently, the black sheep of a family full of goats. Don't ask me what that means—it's what my mom says every year when one of Margaret's handmade Christmas cards lands in our mailbox.

The thing about Margaret is that she's eccentric. I like eccentric. Eccentric usually means fun, and God knows I could use a little of that these days. But according to my family, eccentric translates to trouble. When she was fourteen, Margaret ran away from home because she wanted to join the circus—literally, the circus. *The circus.* They found her mucking horse manure on a farm outside of Kansas City, trying to earn her way to California. Apparently, she'd abandoned her dream of the circus and was now on her way to Hollywood to become the next Shirley Temple— or, at least, Shirley Temple's big sister. She made it out to Los Angeles when she turned eighteen, spent two years working as an extra in films, then returned to the city, rented an apartment with her mother, and spent the next few years as a clerk at a department store until she eloped to Niagara Falls with her boyfriend.

"Traveled the world, honey," she told me at the rehearsal dinner. "That's what I did. That's what you should do, too. You can't claim to live until you do something that makes you feel alive."

"Margaret, you can't say those things to her," my mom had scolded.

"Why the hell not?" Margaret asked, defiance shining in her eyes.

"She means because of this," I said, pulling down the tube sock on my arm to show her my PICC line protected beneath it.

"Bullshit." Margaret waved her hand. "If there's ever a reason to keep dreaming and then go out and do it, that's it."

Like I said, I like Margaret. Everyone else likes to tiptoe around my illness with their false sympathy and high falsetto voices like it's something to be afraid of, but she looks at it straight on. No one else has had the guts to do that—not even my own family.

So when Aunt Mildred-Margaret corners me in the courtyard on the way into the ballroom after cocktail hour, I find I'm almost grateful.

"Which groomsman have you got your eye on?" she asks, nudging me in the shoulder. She doesn't have to bend down too far to talk to me—her back has curved with age, and she pushes a metal walker to help her maintain her balance. But when I look at her, somehow I can only see her as she looked in the pictures she's shown me—tall and blonde and old-Hollywood gorgeous.

"None," I say. "They're all assholes."

"Even the tall one on the right?"

"He's banging Princess Jasmine. And Ariel."

Her eyes widen in surprise, an impish smile on her wrinkled face. "Is that right? And how about that one?" She points a crooked finger at Nathan, who's standing in a corner of the room near the candy bar, glancing nervously around like he's in search of someone. "Is he sleeping with the bridesmaids, too?"

"Nope. He's an asshole all on his own."

She raises an eyebrow. "That's your neighbor, yes?"

It's my turn to be surprised. "How'd you know?"

"Your father mentioned he was your escort tonight."

I snort. "Not likely. Wait—you talked to my dad?"

"Sure." She winks. "You and he are the only two in this family I can reasonably tolerate."

"My dad…" I repeat, trying and failing to hide the doubt in my voice.

I don't know why it rubs me the wrong way. Maybe it's the casual way she groups me and my father together, like we have anything at all in common. We don't—except now we have her. I like Margaret, and she likes me. And she also likes my dad, which means I'm supposed to like my dad if we're going to remain in this happy bubble of us against the world, and I don't want to do that. I'm definitely not going to do that.

"Your dad's a good man. He's a free spirit like us, has an open mind—unlike your mother, I'm afraid."

There it is. Bubble popped.

I whirl around to face her. "My mom has held my hand through every blood draw and biopsy for the past two years while my dad's banged everyone who works for him, including the woman he's with right now. I don't give a fuck about his free spirit."

It would have been a great exit—raised voice, soaring rhetoric—had it not been for the fact that my wheelchair got stuck on the threshold to the ballroom. So there we stand, me with my wheelchair and Aunt Margaret with her walker—nothing in common but broken branches on a family tree and a longing to be anywhere but here.

"I hated my father for abandoning my mother when she got sick," Margaret says, inching her way towards the entrance. "He was the reason I had to come back and take care of her in that shithole on Harker Street." She pauses but doesn't look back at me—just keeps staring straight ahead. I get the sensation that she's been staring straight ahead for most of her life. "But I'll tell you one thing, my only regret is I never got to say thank you for that. I wouldn't trade those last few years with my mother for the world."

She disappears into the ballroom, most likely to camp out near the open bar, and I'm left alone in the courtyard feeling strangely melancholy despite the music and chatter.

"We can't have you hanging out here all night," a voice behind me says. A second later, I feel myself being rolled inside, and I look over my shoulder to see Kurt with a grin on his face, Allison waiting in the doorway for her grand entrance.

"Sorry if I was in your way," I reply tersely, and then instantly regret it. Kurt's smile fades like I've actually stung him.

"You're never in the way," he says.

I sigh and murmur an apology, expecting Kurt to join his bride so they can be introduced properly, but he kneels down in front of me, his eyes soft and full of earnest.

"I grew up with three brothers, but I gotta tell you, Lila, you're the little sister I always wished I had. I'm glad we're family now."

It's the nicest thing he could have said to me, and I feel my eyes welling with unwilling tears.

"You're good for her," I say finally. It feels like something's changing tonight, like peace is being made. I can't even remember why I've held such antipathy towards him for all these years, and now I want to meet him where he is. I want to make everything right. "And I guess, if I have to have a brother-in-law, I'm glad it's you."

Kurt's smile brightens, and I think, *I did that*. And it makes me feel happy to know that just a few words could create this benevolence between us. He leans in to kiss me on the cheek and pats my hand. "Save me a dance later, you got it? I gotta go do the husband thing now."

I nod and watch him jog back to Allison. He whispers something in her ear and she glances at me, then smiles and places a palm on his cheek and kisses him.

"Hey, hey!" The DJ shouts into the microphone while music swells. "We've got plenty of time for that. Let's welcome the new Mr. and Mrs…"

I feel him at my side before I see him, before he speaks. I don't know how I can do that. It's like I have some sixth sense when it comes to him. But there he is, standing just to my right as Allison and Kurt walk into the ballroom holding hands and grinning like lovesick idiots.

"What'd he say to you?" Nathan asks.

I shrug. "Nothing particular."

"But you're smiling."

"Well, it's a wedding, not a funeral."

"I thought you hated him."

"I don't hate anyone tonight."

"Even me?"

If I didn't know any better, I'd say there was hope in his voice. I glance up at him. He's looking down at me, a lock of dark hair falling over his forehead. "Give it time. I'm sure it'll correct itself."

He fights back a smirk as I turn my chair around. "Dance with me later?" he asks.

"You'll have to get in line," I say and wheel myself towards the carving station.

I don't dance with him later. I never get the chance.

Chapter Thirty-Six

"There she is!" My mother coos when I enter the living room. "Doesn't she look beautiful, Frank? Frank." She swats him in the chest. "Tell your daughter she looks beautiful."

My father looks up from his newspaper and smiles. "You do, honey. You look beautiful."

"Okay, now turn around. Go on, twirl." My mother makes a circular motion with her finger, and I roll my eyes and do what I'm told, ever the dutiful daughter. "I knew that dress would be perfect. Didn't I say that dress would be perfect?"

I hate the fact that my mother is right, so I don't say anything. But she is. And it is. The dress is perfect. A light purple chiffon gown with a cinched, beaded bodice, the dress is light and airy and exactly as romantic as I could have dreamed.

"How much did this perfect dress cost me?" Dad asks, but my mom waves him away.

"Never mind that," she says. "This is your daughter's prom. This is going to be the best night of her life."

I don't tell my mom, who never went to her prom, that it probably won't be the best night of my life. In fact, I could hardly care less about going to prom—where the music will suck and the punch will be spiked and Jessica and Amanda will spend the entire night in the bathroom because they lost Prom Queen to, predictably, Gretchen Kelly. What I do care about is this dress, because I feel beautiful in it, and my date, because he makes me feel beautiful, too.

"He's here!" my mom squeals, peeking through the front curtains. "Oh, he looks handsome."

"Mom!" I hiss, but I run to her side and sneak a look beside her. "He does look good in a tux, doesn't he?" We watch him walk up the sidewalk. "What's he got in his hands?"

"That's your corsage, of course!"

"Oh, of course."

We jump back from the window as he approaches the door. A second later, the doorbell rings.

"Hold on, hold on," my dad says, closing his newspaper and putting down his glasses. "I want to meet this young man."

"Dad, you've met him a thousand times before."

"Not on prom night, I haven't."

My mom and I exchange looks. "Come on," she says, placing her hands on my shoulders and steering me into the kitchen. "Let's touch up your hair."

We can hear my dad greeting my date at the door, then the low murmur of voices as they talk about—actually, I don't think I want to imagine what they talk about. When I step into the foyer a few minutes later, he's shifting nervously from foot to foot, but he has a smile on his face.

"Wow." His eyes rake over my body, and I blush. "You look great, Lila."

I suddenly feel shy, and I don't know why. I try to shake the nerves off and point to the plastic container in his hand. "Is that for me?"

He glances down at it, then hurries to open it. "Yeah, it's a white orchid. The lady at the flower shop said it would go with your dress... That's—that's what she said."

"It's beautiful," I say and hold my hand out for him to place it on my wrist. "Thank you."

My mom is glancing back and forth between the two of us, a confused expression on her face, like she's trying to see something there that isn't. I don't know what she's thinking. I don't bother to ask. "It's a very lovely corsage, Dan," she finally says, but her words sound too forced, like she's fitting a puzzle piece into the wrong slot.

"Okay," my dad says, clapping Dan on the shoulder. "Let's take some pictures."

A dozen smiles later and we're walking down the driveway to his car—a '78 Mustang he's bought and restored himself.

"We're going to have fun," Dan says with a smile, opening the passenger door for me.

"Probably not," I say. "But it'll be nice to try."

Dan laughs and shakes his head. "I never know what to make of you, Lila."

He's not the only one.

Our prom is held in the grand ballroom of the luxury hotel downtown—the same ballroom, coincidentally, where my sister is married. Nearby, in the open-air courtyard, some of my classmates are gathered in groups, taking pictures and admiring each other's dresses, but we're being ushered inside by our teachers who drew the short stick and couldn't be less thrilled about serving as chaperones for the evening.

"It looks nice," Dan comments over the din of the music.

And it does. Arches of gold, white, and blue balloons outline the dance floor while large round tables with navy tablecloths line the perimeter. On the right side of the ballroom, a buffet is set up, and some of the football players are already piling their dishes with slices of ham and an assortment of cold salads while their dates admire the desserts.

"Want something to drink?"

I nod and tell him I'm going to find our table, then point to the left so he knows where I'll be.

It's not much different than school. Friends request to sit with friends, and it ends up being exactly like lunchtime in the cafeteria. I'm not saying I mind it—it certainly makes it easier to know where you belong—but it strikes me as disappointing that we can't, for one night, shed our expectations of each other.

I weave my way through the maze of tables, glancing at the name cards and smiling at those I know from class. I see Jessica and Amanda's names and pause, wondering for a brief minute if I'm sitting with my old elementary-school friends, but no—their table is made up of the theater crowd.

"You're with me," a familiar voice says in my ear. I don't have to turn around to know who it is.

"Actually, I'm with him." I point to Dan, who's on the other side of the room talking to one of the football players.

Nathan blinks. "I meant the table, Lilac," he says finally, and I feel my cheeks grow red for the second time tonight. "We're over here."

I follow him two tables over, and sure enough, there's my name in scrawling script on the place setting. The chairs are empty.

"Where's your date?" I ask, removing my wrap and placing my handbag on the table. Nathan's eyes linger on my dress for a moment too long before he swallows and runs a hand through his hair.

"She's with the Bobbsey Twins."

He means Jessica and Amanda—an old nickname that never really stuck except for him and the fact that it's true. Ever since the fourth grade, Jessica and Amanda have been practically glued at the hip.

I follow his gaze across the dance floor and, sure enough, I see them dancing with Christine Blythe, Senior Class President.

"Chrissy?" I ask. "You came with Chrissy?"

He raises an eyebrow and crosses his arms. "What's wrong with Chrissy?"

I shrug my shoulders and pick at the tablecloth. "Nothing. I just didn't think you were into her."

It takes a long time for him to answer. When he does, his words are measured. "Is this gonna be a long night, Lilac?"

"No," I say.

Probably.

"Good. Cause Chrissy's a great person. And you're here with my best friend, so—"

"Because he asked me."

"What?"

"He asked me," I repeat myself. "I'm here with him because he asked me."

He's staring at me. Those dark eyes locking on mine like he can see right through me. I don't know what he's seeing, can't tell what he's thinking. I hate that I never can tell what he's thinking.

"You were waiting for me," he says plainly. I don't answer. "Lilac—" He takes a step closer. "Were you waiting for me?"

"Yo, they have little quiches!" Dan exclaims, walking up behind us. He has two glasses of punch and a dish of hors d'oeuvres balanced in his hands. "I brought some for us to share."

I grab two mini quiches and stuff them in my mouth, if only to stop myself from saying anything stupid.

The night drones on predictably. Dan and I dance during the slow songs then roam the buffet tables during the rest. I try to ignore them, but I find my gaze wandering over to Nathan and Christine, where she rests her head a little too comfortably on his shoulder, where he holds her a little too close around the waist. I look away.

The crowd begins to thin around eleven. Hotel staff carry the empty food platters away on carts, and the few couples lingering on the dance floor sidestep their way around balloons that have come loose from the arches.

"Bartlett's having a post-prom party at his house," Dan says as I gather my wrap and handbag. "Do you wanna go?"

I'm scanning the ballroom for Nathan and Christine, but it's been hours since I've seen them.

"I don't know. Maybe. Who else is going?" We make our way through the courtyard and out into the parking lot.

"Probably the regular crowd," he says and starts to list names.

"What about—what about Christine?"

"I dunno. Probably. Hey…" He tugs gently on my wrap, bringing me to a stop. His smile is shy and warm, lit by the afterglow of the night. "I had a really great time tonight."

His fingers dance with my own, lacing together and unwinding and then wrapping around my hand, pulling me forward. Nathan's forgotten. It's Dan that's here. Dan with the kind smile and soulful eyes. Dan who brought me a white orchid and said I looked great and danced with me at prom.

Dan who I'm kissing right now, in the middle of the hotel parking lot.

I don't know why it feels so wrong.

When we pull away, he's grinning, and he reaches behind me and opens the passenger door. "So," he says. "CJ's?"

"Actually, I'm pretty tired. I think I'm just going to go home." I watch his face fall, and I want to say something to make him smile again, but I don't have it in me. I don't know what's wrong with me, and I just need to be alone to figure it out. Besides, if Nathan is at the post-prom party with Christine, he's the last person I want to encounter while my feelings for Dan are in doubt.

We drive home in relative silence, save for his rhythmic tapping on the wheel to a song only he can hear. He seems to be thinking about something, but I don't dare ask him what. When we pass Nathan's house, I lean forward to look out the window. His truck is in the driveway. I exhale a breath I hadn't realized I was holding.

Dan turns into my driveway and shifts into park. My house is dark, save for the downstairs hall light. My parents have already gone to bed. I find myself glancing up at Nathan's room, at his window that sits opposite mine. The blinds are drawn.

"Is it Nathan?" Dan's voice startles me more than his question, like for a split second I'd forgotten where we were, that he was there. He's looking at me—there's frustration etched on his face, but his tone isn't accusatory. If anything, he sounds defeated. "It is, isn't it?"

"No," I say. And then, because I need him to understand, I say it again more firmly. "No, not at all."

"It's just, you guys used to be close once—"

"That was ages ago, eons ago…"

"—and I saw the way he was looking at you tonight."

Now I really am surprised. "The way he was looking at me? You've got to be joking. The only time Nathan looks at me is when I'm literally in his way. Believe me, it's not like that."

"That's where I think you're wrong," Dan says, and there's a sadness in his eyes now, like maybe he'd hoped he was wrong, too. "I think it's exactly like that."

I don't know what to say. There's a part of me that wants to grab the lapels of his tux and pull him towards me and kiss him, show him he's wrong. There's a part of me that want to tell him, "Forget it. Let's go to CJ's party and have some fun." There's a part of me that wants to rewind the past ten minutes and start again. There's a part of me that's ready to say goodbye.

There's too many parts of me. I don't know how this ends.

He ends it for me. He sighs and leans over, presses his lips against my cheek, then shifts the car into reverse. "I had a really good time with you tonight, Lila," he says, a small smile painting his lips. "I'm not gonna forget it."

I don't know why I'm crying as I gather my things and step out of his car. I don't know why there are tears spilling down my cheeks as I watch him back out of my driveway, watch his taillights disappear down the street. But suddenly I'm sad... Sad like I've just let go of something honest.

I swipe at the tears on my cheeks and turn towards the house.

"Lilac."

His voice is so soft, I almost don't hear him, but when I look up, he's standing on his porch. He's not wearing his tuxedo jacket or vest, and his bowtie is draped loose around his neck. He looks good, even like that. I can see why Christine went out with him.

"Good night?" I call across the yard.

He closes his door and begins walking towards me. I hesitate, start up the driveway towards my house, then close my eyes, say a prayer, and stride across the grass. We pause a few feet away from each other, standing on our own properties like we're marking our territories, and in between us is no-man's land. Who knows who's going to make the first move to claim it. This is anybody's game.

"That was Dan?" he asks.

I nod. "And Chrissy?"

A smirk lifts the corner of his mouth. "She's not here, if that's what you mean."

"It's not."

It is.

"My parents are inside."

"Well... Tell them I say hello."

"Lilac..."

"What!" I explode. "What do you want me to say to you right now? I went to the prom with Dan, and you went with Chrissy, and so what."

"So, I need to know." He takes a step closer. "I need to know if you were waiting for me to ask you."

I bite my lip. I'm not going to lose it in front of him—not here, not now, not tonight. He takes another step closer. I stare at the ground, afraid to look at him. He's inches away, and I can feel him there, like the small space between us is charged with magnetic energy and it would only take one gentle nudge to draw us together. I want to pull away. I want to move forward. I'm afraid of what I really want.

"Were you waiting for me?" he asks again.

"It doesn't matter anymore, does it?"

"Yeah, it does." He reaches behind him, pulls something out of his back pocket. When I glance down, he's holding a pin corsage made of a pale purple lilac and sprig of baby's breath.

I inhale sharply, suddenly aware of everything around me. I can hear crickets in the garden bed, the light wind brushing against the leaves overhead. Dew is already clinging to the grass, and the condensation has started to soak into my shoes.

And Nathan's standing in front of me, holding a flower that was meant for me, eyes boring into my heart. He's asking questions I don't want to answer. Offering answers I'd give anything to hear.

"Lilac—"

"Yes," I breathe, and suddenly his arms are around me, his face nuzzled in my hair. I relax against him, wrap my arms around his back as he holds me tighter. "Yes, I wanted you to ask me."

"Jesus, Lilac," he's saying over and over. "Jesus... Didn't you know? I've been waiting all this time for you."

I'm crying now. Not because of what he's said or what's happened tonight. I'm crying because my mom was right— prom is the best night of my life.

And I'll never get to see it.

Chapter Thirty-Seven

LILAC

16 YEARS, 8 MONTHS

My mother doesn't knock on the door to my room anymore when she comes to check on me. In fact, it's never even closed. I'm fourteen again today, and thinking about what life would be like if I were that teenager who slams doors and blasts emo music and lies in her bed, sulking because her best friend didn't invite her to a party or the cute boy in history class ignored her at school.

But life isn't like that for me, even though I'm fourteen. Maybe it's not really like that for anyone because people are always more complicated than the stereotype. Besides, there's more than one way to tell a story. I've learned that lesson already.

Maybe I just wish that had been my life at fourteen—if I'd had a best friend and a crush on the cute boy in my history class. Maybe I wish I could have been that teenager who fights with her parents all the time and locks herself in her room when she's upset, but I don't know if she ever existed. At least, she doesn't exist in my world. My world when I'm fourteen is filled with emergency rooms and doctor visits, and now doors stay open so my mom can hear me when I need to use the bathroom.

That's how it starts. When I'm fourteen.

I'm fourteen again today, but today it's different. It's getting harder and harder for me to walk now, and twice I've fallen getting out of bed because my legs are weaker than I expect them to be. I can't tell you how much of a pain in the ass that is—when your body doesn't want to listen to what you're telling it to do.

There's an old wheelchair I use to get around upstairs. Mom borrowed it from the church and has it parked near my bedside. My own wheelchair is sitting in a corner in the living room for when I'm feeling strong enough to go downstairs. I don't get out of the house too much any-more—only to the health center and once or twice to the pharmacy—but I like the illusion that I could, if I wanted to.

My mother's going to mass twice a week now. A few times, she stayed behind for the second service, calling Mrs. Emery to come over and stay with me, "just in case." Those "just in case" moments are always awkward. Once, I couldn't make it to the bathroom in time, and it took Mrs. Emery twenty minutes to figure out why I was gradually stuffing my bedcovers underneath me.

"Why didn't you say something?" she'd asked.

Because I thought I still had some pride left. Turns out, I really don't.

Mrs. Emery was a champ and helped me into the chair while she changed my sheets without a complaint. Maybe that's what happens when you're a mom—nothing seems to phase you.

It wasn't so bad after that. Mrs. Emery would make lunch, which was usually canned soup—a pretty safe bet since she's a pretty terrible cook—and we'd watch movies and talk until my mom came home. We tiptoed around any conversation about Nathan, but every so often, he'd filter into our thoughts. My mom told me that he moved out right after Allison's wedding, and I imagined him living in New York City or California, or wherever minors go when they emancipate themselves. But Mrs. Emery let it slip once that he was living with his oldest sister on the other side of town, and the knowledge that he was still so close hurt worse than any of the physical pain I was in at the time. We didn't talk about him after that.

My mom's at church again this morning. Mrs. Emery offered to stay upstairs with me and watch a movie, but the windows are open—I can smell hamburgers on the barbecue a few doors down and hear the hollers of kids playing in the street—and I just want to close my eyes and imagine I'm there with them, riding bikes or running through sprinklers or lounging on a patio eating hamburgers and soaking up the rays of the sun like I used to do when I was younger and healthier and not confined to this bed.

Summer is my favorite season.

I'm dreaming I'm swimming in Gretchen Kelly's pool when I feel my mom's hand on my forehead. It pulls me from a twilight sleep, and I groggily ask her what she's doing.

"Your face is flushed," she says. She opens the drawer in my nightstand and roots past old vitamin bottles until she comes up with a thermometer. "Under your tongue, right now," she commands.

I think I roll my eyes, but I'm so tired, I may have just imagined it.

"How long have you been like this?" she asks, and I raise my eyebrows because she knows I can't answer with a thermometer in my mouth. She clucks her tongue, hands on her hips, and waits impatiently for it to beep. When it does, she glances at the reading and exhales slowly. "Ninety-nine-eight," she recites. "Okay, but if it goes any higher, we're going straight to the hospital."

I nod and lean back against the pillows. I know the drill.

My mom wanders into my bathroom. I hear a cabinet open and close, then the spray of water. A few seconds later, she comes back out with a glass of water, an aspirin, and a cool washcloth. I take them without argument. Some days, I don't have enough fight in me.

My mom pulls the armchair closer to the bed and sits down. "You were sleeping?"

"I was dreaming."

"Was it a good dream?" I nod, and she smiles and brushes my hair out of my eyes. "Good. You should only ever have good dreams."

There's something in these words, in the sound of her voice, that makes me wish my body would cooperate—like I could will my fever to go down and my organs to function and my cells to repair themselves—just for her. Because when I look at her now, I can see how much she's aged in even the past few months—probably more than she'd care to admit. There are dark circles now, a dull glaze in her eyes, like some of her fire has burned out, too. Her auburn hair has faded, wisps of gray layered in the strands. She hasn't dyed it in a while—or cut it, by the looks of it.

"You should go to the hairdresser tomorrow," I tell her.

She raises an eyebrow and sits up, patting her hair. "Why, do I look that terrible?"

"No. You look beautiful." This surprises her more than anything, and her eyes glisten with unshed tears.

"Well," she says after a moment. "Maybe I'll make an appointment. Can't have myself looking slovenly next to Joanne Emery, now can I?"

"She doesn't even compare."

My mom smiles and takes the washcloth from me, placing a hand against my cheek to test my temperature the way only moms know how. "You're a sweet liar, aren't you?"

We sit there in that silence for a while. The TV is on downstairs—some comedy in syndication on one of those cable channels. I'm trying to make out which one, but all I hear is the canned laughter from the audience laugh tracks. I wish I knew what was so funny. I'd love to laugh again. But it's like the longer this goes on, the heavier this illness seems to weigh, and I forget what it feels like to even smile.

I watch my mom watch me. She's been bearing this weight, too, for far too long.

"Are you scared?" I ask quietly.

My mom nods slowly. "I'm terrified."

I don't have the words to tell her it's going to be okay. I don't have those promises to make. So I do the only thing I can for her.

"I want to go for a walk outside," I say.

"Are you sure? It's starting to get cool out—"

"I know. But I want to feel the air. I want to use my legs when I can. I want to try."

I don't give up.

Chapter Thirty-Eight

All I need is fresh air. Really, that's the only reason why I run out into the courtyard—lit up by white Christmas lights that I'm sure to someone seemed romantic, but to me seems like a pretty fast way to run up the electric bill.

Inside the ballroom, family and friends chat and toast and clink their butter knives against champagne flutes until Allison and Kurt kiss and everyone else cheers. My mom stays close to me for most of dinner until I insist she mingle with family—just keep away from Aunt Mildred-Margaret—but it isn't until she realizes we have four nurses in the family that she lets herself stop being my mom for a while and start being Allison's.

"What do you think?" Kurt appears from behind me, leaning his elbows on the table as he surveys the dance floor. "You ready to get this party started?"

He helps me stand, and soon we're abandoning my wheelchair and walking out onto the dance floor where Allison is already swaying with Dad. She smiles at me, and for the first time since they started planning their wedding, I feel wanted, feel included, feel like I'm not just a placeholder bridesmaid because I'm her little sister, like I'm not just a nuisance because I've been sick.

"You doing okay?" Kurt asks, and I nod as we continue to sway to a slow song about looking wonderful tonight. I want to be present. I want to make a memory of this. I want to remember what it feels like to dance later. But my eyes keep sweeping across the room, looking for Nathan, because all I can think about is how he had called me beautiful. *Beautiful.* I haven't felt beautiful in forever.

"Mind if I cut in?"

It's not who I expect. It's definitely not who I want to dance with. But my dad has his arms outstretched expectantly, and Kurt is already whisking Allison away, glancing back with a grin and a wink.

I want to kill him. Any goodwill he's recently earned is shattered by his abandonment, this deception that has left me alone with my dad.

My dad mistakes my hesitation. "Are you not well? Do you need me to get your mother?"

I roll my eyes. That's his answer for everything when it comes to me. God help him if he had to take care of me himself.

"No, Dad. I'm fine."

I place my hand in his, and for a moment my breath catches. His hand is rough and calloused and still large around mine, and I'm reminded of all those times I used to climb in his lap and beg him to read me a bedtime story, all those times he brushed the tangles out of my hair before school, all those times he reached for my hand to stop me from running across the street to the merry-go-round. He was my dad when I needed him then, and remembering that—remembering how he was always there—stabs at my heart and makes tears well in my eyes. Because he's not that man anymore. He hasn't held my hand since then, even though I still need him now.

Tears are pricking at the corners of my eyes, and I slip my hand from his and duck my head so he doesn't see.

"I need my wheelchair," I mutter and run away as fast as I can, past the dining tables and out into the courtyard.

The exertion is too much, and I bend over, clutching my abdomen, sucking in large mouthfuls of air. But I'm breathing too hard, my heart is racing too fast, and soon the white Christmas lights blur and the world tilts and turns, and I feel my knees buckling.

Someone's at my side, their hands on my waist, holding me up and guiding me three steps to a cast iron bench where I collapse and keep my head bent low.

"What do you need?" Nathan asks through the roaring in my ears. I close my eyes to make the room stop spinning.

"I need my wheelchair. And my dad."

I don't want my mom to see me like this. Not like this, not on Allison's wedding day. I want her to have happy memories of at least one daughter. And besides, my dad doesn't get the dances but not the dying. Let him deal with this for a while.

To his credit, his face is full of concern when he sees me, and he rushes to my side and places a gentle hand on my back. "What do you need?" he echoes Nathan. "Should I get Mom?"

Mom, he says. Not "your mother" like he usually does. Mom. Like they're still a unit. Like we're still a family.

"No, don't get Mom," I say. "I just need to go home and rest." I look up and catch him exchanging glances with Nathan, see their doubt, and I sigh and force a smile. Somehow, I can never be bitter and resentful for long, no matter how much I want to. "See?" I say, trying to diffuse the situation. "I'm fine. I just overdid it when I was dancing with Kurt, and now I need to sleep."

My dad scratches his beard, then nods. "Okay, we'll get you home."

"I'll take her," Nathan offers.

Dad raises his eyebrows. "Are you sure?"

"Sure—I'll stick the wheelchair in the back of the truck again. No problem."

"And you can be home alone?" Doubt is creeping back into my dad's voice. I can tell he wants to run back into the ballroom and find my mother so this responsibility is out of his hands.

"I'll hang around," Nathan says.

For the first time in years, I'm grateful for Nathan Emery. It's not the last.

Chapter Thirty-Nine

The earliest memory I have is of my dad. I wish that wasn't true. He doesn't deserve my first memory. But there I am, four years old and holding his hand as I skip along beside him, eager to see the new playground that's been erected a few blocks from our house.

"This used to be only fields, you know," my dad says. "Cornfields and trees. Now look—a brand new park for you kids to play in."

Except Allison's too old to play at the park. So now it's just me and him.

I like it that way, I remember that much. Because this was before—before he started screwing around on my mom and abandoned our family. Before I got sick and he abandoned me. Before... When he was still the dad I needed. The dad I wanted him to be.

"There's a merry-go-round and everything," he says, and I look up at him with wide eyes and a big smile. "You're gonna love the merry-go-round, Lilac. We'll plop you right in the center and spin you around and around..."

It's a fall day. The end of September, I think. It must be because the leaves are turning orange and I'm wearing a purple jacket that itches at the collar. I remember the jacket because as soon as we get to the park, my dad lets me take it off and spreads it out in the middle of the merry-go-round. I lay on top of it and stare up at the clouds in the sky, watching the world spin around and around and around, just like he said it would.

We play for hours, months, years on that fall day in the park. On swings, on slides, on jungle gyms. When it's time to leave, I take his hand, and we begin to retrace our footsteps. I look back, see my jacket laying there on the merry-go-round, waiting for me to hurry back and claim it as mine.

I don't say anything.

I never see that purple jacket again.

Chapter Forty

It's not the pain that bothers me so much, though my insides feel like they're burning and every inch of me aches down to the bone. It's not even how lightheaded I feel—like I'm still in the ballroom dancing, twirling and swirling and caught a bit off-balance. No, it's the damn fatigue. I can feel myself sinking under the weight of it, the fog in my mind growing so thick, I can't see straight.

But it's not even the fatigue itself that gets to me...

It's how much I'm missing because of it.

I suppose I'll have to get used to it. Those woods might be lovely, dark, and deep, Robert Frost, but hell, those miles are coming up on us fast.

"You cold?" Nathan asks, and I lift my head from where it's resting against the window and shake my head.

"Little warm, actually." His eyes sweep across my face, and I swear I see his hand leave the steering wheel for a split-second before his grip tightens again. "It's okay," I assure him. "I just need to get home to rest. Too much champagne, I guess." I try to crack a smile, but even that hurts, and I lean my head back against the passenger seat.

Outside, the rain is starting to grow heavy, and Nathan flicks his windshield wipers into a higher gear. The rhythm of rain on the roof and the swish of the wipers create a sort of lullaby I think I could fall asleep to, but I'm struggling to stay awake. I want to stay awake, I want to stay awake… I don't want to go to sleep just yet.

"It looks so pretty," I murmur, so quietly I don't think he hears me. But after a moment, he says,

"What does?"

I nod at the road ahead of us, darkened by both the night and the rainstorm. Every so often, when we pass a strip of stores with neon blue and green signs, the light will stretch across the slick pavement, and for a moment it feels like we're driving across oceans.

"It's like the world is glowing." I turn my head to look at him. "What do you see?"

He keeps his eyes steady on the road. "I see puddles and potholes, and that's about it."

"Anyone ever tell you you're no fun?"

"Pretty sure everyone tells me that." He flips on his turn signal, moves into the adjacent lane and stops at a red light. It's only then that he turns to look at me, and I'm so taken aback by the sincerity in his eyes, I sit up. "It was a nice wedding."

"Yeah…"

"I'm glad I came."

"Well, you were invited."

"I mean, I'm glad I came with you."

"Oh."

"Yeah."

"Green light."

"What?"

I point at the traffic light. "The light's green."

"Oh."

"Yeah."

We turn left and drive past the high school, past the Starbucks and the park. Trees line the sidewalks on either side of us, their branches bridging telephone wires, and narrow plots of land are broken up by driveways that lead to Cape Cods long since decorated for Christmas.

Nathan clears his throat. "My dad didn't forget to pick up the wedding gift," he finally says. "I know I said that, but it wasn't true." He pauses, sweeps a hand through his hair, jabs at the radio button on the dashboard so music fills the cab, then shuts it back off again. I watch him, waiting for him to continue, wondering where we're headed in this conversation. Wondering if we'll come back from it.

"The truth is... Truth is, he broke it. The vase, I mean. It was a vase—crystal or some shit. And he broke it. Dropped it and passed out when he was picking up the pieces. My mom found him with his hands all cut up."

"Oh, God," I breathe. "Was he okay, did he—"

"He was drunk, Lilac." He clenches his jaw, tightens his grip around the steering wheel as he fights for control. "He was fucking black-out drunk and bleeding all over the living room."

"What about your mom?" I ask quietly.

"I don't know." He shakes his head. "I don't know... She makes excuses for him. He'll go away for a while, claim he's getting sober, then come back and fuck up again. She always has an excuse."

I think back to the day I came home from the hospital the first time—the day we saw Mrs. Emery jogging and my dad made a comment about Mr. Emery always being away. We all assumed Mr. Emery was cheating on his wife. Turns out my dad is that kind of bastard. But Mr. Emery...

I glance at Nathan. He's staring straight ahead, the muscles in his jaw twitching.

Mr. Emery might be something else.

"I can't do it." His voice is so quiet, I have to strain to hear him, even in the relative silence of the truck cab. "I can't sit back and watch her pretend everything's fine when he's destroying her, destroying me, destroying himself."

The words surprise me. "Does he—I mean, has he—"

"Once. But he was so far gone, he took one swing and was flat on the floor." He puts on his turn signal, a rhythmic clicking sound that beats in time with the rain, and turns into our neighborhood. When he speaks again, his voice is calmer, quieter. "Anyway, it doesn't always take a fist to land a punch."

I don't know what to say. "I didn't know."

"No," he says with some relief in his voice, like maybe he's grateful for that much. "Isn't that the point? Does anyone ever?"

He turns down our street, and I watch familiar houses pass by in a blur. Bay windows are embellished with colorful packages and sleds and Santa Claus statues, and through open curtains, I can see Christmas trees trimmed and waiting patiently for their moment to shine. Multi-colored Christmas lights decorate bushes and bare tree branches and porch trim in a festive display, tempered only by a blanket of rain instead of the expected snow. Ahead on the left, I know my own house will be dark in contrast. It's a week before Christmas, but I think this year we'll be lucky if we even get a tree.

"I know things have been weird between us," I begin, turning to him suddenly. "Nate, if you need—"

But Nathan's not paying any attention. Instead, he's leaning forward, peering out the windshield. "What the…"

He flicks on his high beams, and I follow his gaze. The Emery's sedan is parked across their front lawn, a trail of muddy tire tracks leading from the curb, headlights striking the house at an odd angle. Nathan slams on his brakes and swerves to the side of the road. I gasp, my hand shooting out to steady myself against the dashboard, the seatbelt snapping me back against the seat.

"Fuck." He throws the car into park and turns to me, eyes sweeping over me quickly. "Are you okay?" I nod mutely, if only because I have no idea what's happening right now. "Fuck!" He slams his hand against the steering wheel and throws open his door. "Stay here!" he orders.

Through the open door and sheet of rain, I watch him race across his yard to the car, glance briefly inside the driver's window, then bolt for the house, disappearing through the front door. The pressure grows in my chest as I wait for him, knowing what he's just confided in me, knowing what this could mean. I didn't know it was this bad, didn't know this is what his life had been like just next door.

I want to take it all back—every snarky comment that has earned me one of his infamous smirks, every "I hate you" that I only half-mean, and doesn't he know it. I want him to know I'm sorry for all those years ago, that I forgive him for that one day we don't talk about, if only it will make tonight, right now, go away.

I glance at the sedan parked haphazardly across the lawn and unbuckle my seatbelt. The hem of my dress becomes submerged in a puddle as I slide out of the truck and step onto the curb. My shoes sink into soft grass, and I wrap my coat tighter around me as the rain pounds at my back, my hair unraveling from their pins and growing heavy by the second. I know what I must look like now, but it's okay. Today was Allison's dream. Not mine.

I open the car door and stick my head in, switching off the headlights and grabbing the keys from the ignition. I'm already halfway up his front walk when he appears in the doorway again, hand outstretched as if to stop me from coming any further.

"He's passed out on the couch."

"Your mom?"

"Not here."

I nod as he shuts the door behind him and steps out from under the porch overhang. Beads of water are dripping from his hair, and he runs a palm across his face. I don't think it's just the rainwater he's trying to make disappear. He stares at me for a moment, like he's processing seeing me there, standing by his family's car in the middle of the yard in a winter rainstorm.

"I've gotta get you home," he says, stepping closer.

"I can make it." I hand him the keys, and he pauses, his hand wrapped around mine.

"Jesus, Lilac, you're shaking."

I am, but I don't know if it's from the cold or the rain or everything that's happening now. There's something in his eyes I've never seen before, something in the way he confided in me on the way home tonight that makes me think he's no longer simply the boy next door. At least, not the boy I thought he was. Standing in front of me is someone I recognize, like I'm looking at my own reflection—someone who knows the gravity of their situation, someone who has lived with their burdens for way too long. Someone who knows that it has to end, if only they could figure out how or when.

I want to tell him it's okay, that I know how he's feeling. I want to tell him that we're friends again, that I'm right next door, that I've always been right next door. It feels like the right words are there, bubbling up to the surface, and if I can grab them, then maybe this all really will turn out okay. But cold truths scatter around us, splattering against the pavement.

I don't have the heart to lie to him tonight.

Chapter Forty-One

I'm six years old today. There are three things I know.

1. My best friend, Kate, has moved out of the house next door.

2. A boy named Nathan has just moved in.

3. From this point on, I'll never remember what life was like without him.

Chapter Forty-Two

EIGHT MONTHS EARLIER

He's already walking across the lawn towards my house by the time I turn to follow. He promised my dad he'd see me home, after all, and damn it, he's going to take care of someone tonight. I know the determined look that's etched across his face, the look he tries to hide behind his casual smiles. He forgets I've known him since we were six.

He's halfway across my driveway when I stop and abruptly turn around, begin walking back in the direction of his house.

"Lilac?" he calls out. "Lilac, what the hell are you doing?"

But I ignore him, step a few more feet, and bend over. Those aren't words that are coming up now.

He's at my side in a second, but I push him away and wipe my mouth with the corner sleeve of my coat. "I didn't want you to see that," I say, my teeth beginning to chatter.

He doesn't say anything. Hand on my back, he ushers me across the yard and up the porch steps to where we can finally find shelter. I flick on the lights as we step through the front door, and he blinks and glances around like he's seeing my house for the first time. I don't blame him. It's been ages since he was last here.

"Your wheelchair," he says, remembering before I do that it's still sitting in the bed of his truck.

He's out the door before I can protest. It's okay. I'm going to need my wheelchair now more than ever. It was too much today. Too much walking. Too much dancing. Too much of everything, and now the energy is draining from my body with every shuffle of my feet, my legs growing weak and my mind becoming heavy like I'm wading through a thick fog. I reach for the bannister and try to pull myself up, but I only make it a single step before I find myself sinking to the carpet. I lean my forehead against the wall, the surface cooling my skin even as my body shakes.

That's where he finds me when he opens the door again, wheeling in puddles of rainwater along with my chair.

"I just need a minute," I murmur, my eyes closed. "Just one minute."

He maneuvers the wheelchair into a corner by the door, then bends down and slides one arm around my waist, helping me to my feet without much effort. I lean against him as we climb the stairs, Nathan carrying the brunt of my weight.

"I told you to stay in the truck," he scolds.

"Yeah, well, you know I always listen to you."

In my room, he helps me out of my coat and tosses it onto the armchair by the closet. My dress is soaked through and cold, and I know how dangerous this is, know I have to get out of my clothes and straight into bed.

We've been down this road before.

The straps of my dress are already halfway down my shoulders before I realize Nathan's still in the room, standing in the doorway to my bathroom with a towel in his hands, eyebrows raised.

"You, uh, need some help?"

There it is, that lingering smirk I know so well. I realize I'm actually relieved to see it.

"Just close your eyes and unhook the back for me."

"You know your room's directly across from mine, right?" he says. "Pretty sure I've already seen everything."

The words are an echo, like I've heard them before, but I can't recall when or where. I feel my cheeks flush, and I turn around so he doesn't see. "You wish, Emery."

I can feel him step closer. I lift my hair, and he unhooks my dress at the nape of my neck, then places the towel in its place. I turn around slowly, acutely aware of how his fingers are lingering on the terrycloth at my shoulders, how they wander down and stop at the protective band of cranberry-colored fabric that's wrapped around my upper arm. His touch burns, even though my body already feels like it's on fire, and I shiver again. He pulls back like he's the one who's been scorched.

"I need to call my mom."

"I need to—" I point to the bathroom, then pick up my flannel pajamas from the bottom of my bed and close the door behind me.

I don't know how long I'm in there. Somehow, I manage to change out of my dress and into my pajamas, which is a welcome relief from the wet clothes, but it doesn't do much to stop the chill or the wave of weakness that comes with it. There's a pounding in my head. There's a pounding on the door.

"My dad left my mom at the reception," I hear Nathan say, though he sounds so far away. "I'm gonna go pick her up." A pause. "Lilac, you hear me?" Another pause, another knock. "Lilac, are you okay?"

I swear I think I'm answering him. I'm moving my lips and everything, but no sound is coming out. Maybe I'm just imagining it. Maybe I'm just imagining him. Maybe I'm imagining that I'm curled in a fetal position in the narrow space between the toilet and the bathtub, my face pressed against the cold tile floor.

I hear the doorknob turn, and then the door nudges open.

"Lilac? Shit!" I open my eyes to see him crouching next to me, face filled with panic. "What's wrong? What do I do?"

"Cold," I murmur. I have the towel wrapped around me like a blanket, covering part of my head. He tugs it down, presses a palm against my forehead. I look up, and his eyes lock on mine, full of concern, full of fear, full of something else I never expected to see from him.

This isn't the Nathan Emery I know.

"Come on," he says and scoops me up, carrying me to the bed where he tucks the blankets around me. He grabs the afghan off the back of the armchair by my closet and layers it on top, then glances around the room, his eyes landing on the medicine and supplement bottles, the packaged syringes and flush kits for my line. "I'm—I'm gonna call your mom, okay?" He swallows and avoids my eyes, reaches over to pick up the phone on my nightstand. He barely holds it up to his ear before the front door flies open, my mother calling my name.

Nathan disappears into the hall, and soon I hear her foot-steps on the stairs. She races into the room, pausing only briefly when she sees me swaddled like a child in my bed.

"What happened?" She rushes over, places a hand against my cheek, my forehead. "Oh, my God, what happened?"

Nathan's standing in the doorway to my room, hands in his pockets, head bowed like he can't stand to look at me anymore. "We got caught in the rain. I'm sorry, it was my fault—"

But my mom isn't listening to him. She's already rooting through the nightstand for the thermometer. "You should have let me know you were taking her home," she says angrily. "You should have called me."

But her reproach is futile. He's already gone.

Now that's the Nathan Emery I know.

Chapter Forty-Three

I'm fifty today. Historically, I would probably be considered ancient, but now that the population of the planet is ballooning and medical innovation is thriving and people are living longer than ever, fifty is considered middle-aged, which means I've got a couple of decades' worth of good years still ahead of me.

I like fifty. It's a strong number, a solid number. Exactly halfway between zero and one hundred, it knows its role, knows it stands in the balance of everything that came before and everything that comes after. Fifty is the midpoint of a life well-lived.

I imagine myself getting laugh lines and sun spots and gray hair when I'm fifty. I imagine stepping onto the scale and wondering where those added pounds came from, looking in the mirror and admiring the expensive new bra that promises extra lift. I imagine my hands—long, slender fingers and manicured nails and prominent veins that give away my age. They're hands that have cooked meals, that have written love letters, that have raised children. They've been there since the beginning. They'll be there in the end.

I love my body at fifty. I love every curve, every wrinkle, every scar. I love them because they're a reminder of where I've been and that I've made it this far.

I wish I could have made it this far.

Chapter Forty-Four

Nathan and I are going to be astronomers. We decide this after a field trip to the high school planetarium, where we learn about constellations and the composite of stars and how to map the phases of the moon. My dad gets me a telescope for my tenth birthday—one of the better things he's ever done—and we're so in awe of it, we're almost afraid to try it out because it's a real telescope and not one of those cheap plastic toys you can get at a big box store.

We set it up in the space between our houses—away from the patio lights and willow trees that pepper the edge of our backyards—and nestle into our winter coats and wool hats, pointing out craters and wondering if that's where the man in the moon lives and marveling how it really does look like Swiss cheese.

For a period of about five seconds, we think about becoming astronauts, about what it would be like to walk on the moon—or Mars—and look down on Earth from space. But then I remind him that time moves differently in space and that the world looks different, too.

"Everyone would be like—like ants," I say, settling into the lawn chair and wrapping my sleeping bag around me like a blanket. "Smaller than ants. Like specks of dust. You wouldn't be able to see or talk to anyone back home." He's quiet as he thinks about this. It doesn't seem to bother him. "And you'd be away for a really long time," I add. "And if something bad happens to the shuttle, you can't ever come back."

This makes him frown. "Ever?"

"Ever."

"Would you be in space with me?"

"I'd be in the command center, trying to figure out a way to get you back."

His eyes light up. "You'd do that?"

"Of course I would. I don't want my best friend lost in space forever."

He smiles and shoves his hands in his pockets. "Good. Because I don't like the sound of forever."

Truth be told, neither do I.

Chapter Forty-Five

Today's my seventeenth birthday, but the day starts out pretty much the same as every other day. I wake up, eat cereal that has way too much sugar in it, and then do the school thing. I wish the school thing was optional by now. I'm ready to think about anything else but History or Anatomy—or the History of Anatomy, or whatever it is we're supposed to be taking our junior year.

It doesn't matter, anyway. It's not what we're here for today. Today, it's all about eyes locking as we pass each other in the hallway, our gazes casually meeting above the cafeteria crowd, a shared relief at seeing the empty desk in English and stolen glances and shy, secret smiles as I slip into the seat beside him.

I'm at my usual desk by the window a full half an hour before homeroom, trying to cram for a History of Anatomy test that'll count for twenty percent of my grade. The halls are starting to fill up as the buses begin to arrive, and pieces of conversation are filtering through the open door. There are a few students in the classroom with me. Christine Blythe is furiously copying notes from her textbook, and CJ Bartlett has his head in his arms and seems to be sound asleep.

I can tell Nathan's there before I even look up. He somehow fills the room, like the air surrounding him becomes electrified, and even CJ opens his eyes long enough to see who's disturbed the force. I glance at Nathan, then turn back to my book, hiding a smile as he maneuvers the desks and slides into the seat behind me. I'm acutely aware of his every move.

He taps me on the shoulder. "Happy Birthday, Lilac Sophia," he says. "I got you something."

I turn around at this, not even bothering to mask my surprise. The last time Nathan got me a present, we were eleven years old, and I swore I never wanted to see him again. If this turns out anything like that, I'd rather he keep his gift and we forget my birthday altogether.

But this isn't then. No, this isn't even real.

"Here," he says, tossing a piece of paper over my shoulder. I stare at it wordlessly, look up at him to make sure he's serious, then glance back at it again.

"You want me to edit your English paper?" I ask him in disbelief. "You realize you're the shittiest gift-giver in the world, right?"

"Yeah, well…" He gestures to his essay. "You're better at this stuff than me."

"Nathan, you're already getting an 'A' in this class."

He leans back in the chair, a faint smile hanging on his lips. "And now I'll be able to maintain that 'A' because you're editing my paper."

I have to admit, I don't have a counterargument. So I shake my head and grab a pen and lean over his desk to skim through the text.

"Okay, well, this 'I' needs to be capitalized," I say, circling the letter in the first paragraph. I look up to see if he's following along, but he's staring out the window. "Are you paying attention?"

"Yep." His smile has faded, and he's drumming his hands on his legs in an erratic rhythm. He quickly glances at me, then looks away.

I shake my head again and continue scanning the page. "You have a duplicate word here—don't forget to delete it." I circle the word "love," then shift my attention back up to the title of the essay. "Wait, what assignment is this?"

"Anything else?"

I keep reading. "I think you probably mistyped this." I draw a circle around "you," then freeze, staring down at the three words that seem to jump off the page. When I look up again, he's grinning.

"Happy Birthday, Lilac Sophia," he says.

I bet I would have really liked seventeen.

Chapter Forty-Six

This is how it happens.

We spend every Saturday night for nearly a year in my backyard looking through my telescope, tracking the movement of the earth along with the shifting seasons, trying to figure out if that glob of light we're having trouble focusing on is a star or a satellite or something even stranger. We keep composition books filled with notes from our teachers and make copies of star charts at the library, giggling with renewed excitement when we locate a constellation, tracing it over and over in the air until we can map it again on our own with ease. For one year, all of our attention is turned towards the stars. Sometimes, when he's not looking, my attention is turned towards him.

If Nathan was my friend before, our friendship is only strengthened the year we turn ten. He eats dinner at our house twice a week, which my mom loves because it means someone finally appreciates her cooking, and then once the dishes are cleared, we do our homework or play a board game or try to see how far our telescope will reach until his mom calls him to come back home. On the weekends in the summer, we drag our sleeping bags out to the backyard and spread them out near the willow trees and the creek that has dried up with the drought, pieces of Velociraptor still buried somewhere beneath its bed. Our telescope aimed towards Mars, we stare up at the night sky, at the stars we've come to know so well, and imagine the stars know us.

When school starts again, we sit together on the bus and partner for experiments and make sure we're on each other's team when we play kickball at recess. The other kids tease us, but that's because they don't understand. We're exploring the universe together. We're partners in science. We're allies in a space war.

We're best friends. When I close my eyes at night, I find myself dreaming that someday we'll be even more than that.

"I got you something."

I pull away from the telescope and stare at him. The light from the patio barely touches us here in the space between our houses, but the moon is full and illuminates the yard. When I speak, I can see my breath cloud and evaporate into the air. "A present?"

"For your birthday."

I grin. "Do I have to wait until the party tomorrow?"

He shakes his head and drags his backpack from behind his lawn chair. I watch him unzip the bag, watch him reach in with both hands. When he pulls them out again, he's holding a package the shape of a large jar. The blue and silver gift wrap is crinkled and ripped and mended again with pieces of tape. I imagine him sitting on the floor of his bedroom, rolls of his mother's wrapping paper stretched out before him, trying to figure out how to wrap my present himself, and something grows warm inside of me to think he didn't want anyone else to do it for him.

He hesitates, glances down at the gift in his hands.

"What's the matter?" I ask.

He shrugs. "I just want to make sure you like it, that's all."

"Of course I'm gonna like it," I say. "I'll like anything you give me." I bite my lip. I didn't mean to say that—not like that, anyway. But he's smiling and holding it out to me, and I grin and take it from him, pause to admire the wrapping again, then rip through the paper. "Whoa!"

"It's a star lamp," he explains as I turn the plastic cylinder over in my hands. Even in the relative darkness, I can make out vague constellations etched into the base. "You plug it in, and it's like you're outside."

We stare at each other for a moment, then we race into the house, calling out to my parents who are watching TV in the living room that Nathan got me a gift we're gonna test out upstairs. I shove aside some books on my desk, and Nathan clears a path to the outlet and plugs in the lamp.

"Ready?" he asks, tossing his coat on the bed.

I nod and flip the light switch. In an instant, my room is filled with a thousand shining stars, projecting onto the walls, the ceiling, the carpet. We're swimming in constellations, so close we can reach up and touch them. So close, I reach my hand out to try.

"This is—"

"Awesome," he finishes, grinning wildly.

His eyes lock on mine, and I feel that warmth building in my stomach again, feel something like butterflies fluttering around in there. We're standing inches apart, the whole of the universe right there in my bedroom because he did that. He brought the stars here for me. My cheeks grow warm, and I lean forward and close my eyes and brush my lips against his.

He jumps back, his eyes wide in alarm. "What'd you do that for?"

I don't expect the anger in his voice, and I back away quickly until I'm leaning against the dresser. "I don't know," I stammer. And I don't. I don't know why I kissed him. It just felt like the kind of thing people do at times like this. "I thought—" He's staring at me, waiting for me to finish. "I thought you liked me."

"You're my best friend," he says, like that's supposed to explain everything.

"But—"

"I like Amanda Zeleski," he says.

"But—"

"And besides, if I knew you were gonna do that, I wouldn't have gotten you the stupid lamp." There's something in those last words that hurt me way more than the others. Maybe not the words themselves, but the way he says them. There's an anger beneath them. A betrayal. Like I've just messed everything up, and now nothing's going to be the same again. He grabs his coat and runs out of the room.

He doesn't come over to chart constellations anymore. We don't sit together on the bus.

The stars never do look the same after that.

Chapter Forty-Seven

I'm in love with Nathan Emery. He doesn't love me back.

FALL

Chapter Forty-Eight

LILAC

16 YEARS, 9 MONTHS

"How are you doing, Lila?"

Dr. Wilhems isn't patronizing when he speaks to me. I like that about him. Even if he knows the truth about how I'm feeling, he always asks, always makes sure to hear it straight from me. He keeps his eyes on me when I'm talking so I know he's really listening. They're kind eyes—the same kind eyes as Nathan, as my mom. They're eyes that tell a story with just one look, stories that share a sense of humor or hope for a happy ending.

That's not the story they're telling today.

"I'm tired," I tell him plainly because I just don't have the energy to say something witty in reply.

I wish I did. I wish I could reply with something snarky because then at least I'd know I was still Lilac underneath all this fatigue and pain, like this illness could take everything else, but it couldn't take away me. But today is one of those days where I don't recognize myself even when I speak. I bet if I looked in the mirror, I wouldn't recognize myself there, either. I'd see just a ghost of a girl staring back, this hollow outline where the real Lilac used to be.

Dr. Wilhems lowers himself into the chair beside me. "I know, sweetheart. I know. How's your appetite?"

"She's eating on and off," my mom answers for me from the doorway. "Sometimes whole meals, sometimes nothing more than broth."

She would know. More and more, I don't have the strength to walk downstairs, so she brings me my meals on a tray. She mostly cooks my favorites now—baked chicken and mashed potatoes, fish tacos, or ravioli and meatballs the way that place on Spruce Street makes them—but I can only eat a few bites at a time, and more than once I've ended up picking apart the tacos without eating a thing. I always feel bad when she realizes this and takes the tray back downstairs. It's not that I don't want to eat. It's just that I barely have enough energy to lift a fork.

"I'm too tired," I explain. I feel ashamed, like maybe I should be trying harder—for me, for her—but I don't know if I have it in me.

"What about those nutritional shakes—the home nurse said they're good for calories."

"Please don't make me drink those," I beg her. "They're terrible. They taste like someone blended up a tub of paste."

"But you have to eat," my mom says. She turns to Dr. Wilhems, desperation creeping into her voice. "She has to eat, right? To keep up her strength?"

"Isn't this doing the job?" I gently tug on my line. Dr. Wilhems' eyes drift upward to check the IV bag that's become a fixture in my bedroom.

"We can make some adjustments, but you just keep doing what you can, okay?" he says comfortingly. "I swiped a couple of pudding cups from the cafeteria for you. How about we try one of those?"

He glances at my mom, who sighs with relief and nods and disappears out the door. I grin at Dr. Wilhems.

"I didn't think I was going to win that round."

He winks. "Moms just like to know they're still needed."

This silences me, strikes something painful in my heart, and I struggle to sit up if only to distract myself from the hot tears that have begun to sting my eyes. I need my mom. I do need her. And not just when she's helping me into the bathroom or bringing me my meals. I need her now because I can't stand to think of the day—months, weeks from now—when I won't need her anymore.

I can see how this is affecting everyone around me now, when I didn't want to think about it before. I can see it when my sister calls my mom, then forwards me cute emails immediately after because she still can't bring herself to talk to me directly—like one of us will break if she says so much as "hey." I see it when my dad drops off care packages filled with movies and books and silly socks that I bet anything Rebecca picked out, when he pokes his head in to say hello and not much else because what else can he say?

I see it especially in my mom. I see it in the way she moves, the way she speaks to me, the way she looks at me. Everything is precise, infused with meaning for her. When we're watching a movie together and I fall asleep, she'll cover me with the blanket her mother made, the afghan that used to be hers, and the movement is enough to wake me up again. It's then that I'll catch her staring at me, her eyes roaming across my face like she's memorizing it, memorizing the moment. When she says goodnight, the word sounds a little heavier, like she never knows if goodnight will mean goodbye.

My mother isn't going to church on Sundays like I thought she was. She's going to a support group for parents of kids like me. Dr. Wilhems introduced her to it a couple of months ago, when I arrived home from the hospital the last time. At first, I was surprised—pissed, even. Because what did it say about my odds if they were already betting against me? But now I'm relieved. If Dr. Wilhems can't save my life, maybe he can save my mom's.

Dr. Wilhems is studying me, but not as a patient or a case study. It's like he sees me—*me*—reminding me that I'm still here. "How are you really doing?" he asks.

"I hate this," I admit to him. "It feels like my body isn't my own anymore. I'm so tired all the time—way more than before. It's like it hurts to stay awake now."

He pats my hand, then turns my wrist over and rests two fingers on my pulse. "Good," he says finally and lowers my hand back to the bed. "Your heart rate's good."

"Awesome. Let's go for a run."

Oh. There I am. It startles me for a minute to hear that side of me come out again, when I thought I'd gotten so lost, I could never find my way back to myself. I've been a stranger in this body for the past few months, and now, here I am—shades of the old Lilac peeking through. Dr. Wilhems smiles like he recognizes me, too, and I exhale slowly and lean back against the pillows. Maybe I'm not so far gone yet.

"Good to see that sense of humor again," he says.

"It's good to have it back again," I tell him. "I thought it was gone for good."

"Nah," he says with a smile. "Underneath the illness, you're still you." He hesitates and glances at the door, then shifts forward on the edge of the seat. "We need to talk about your care, Lila. You need to know you have some options."

I wonder briefly if we're going to wait for my mom to come back because this is the kind of thing doctors discuss with parents in the room. Then I realize I'm old enough today. Maybe when you're the one that's dying, you're always old enough.

"What kind of options?" I ask, but I can see the answer in his eyes. Life-sustaining options, not life-saving ones. "I don't want to go back to the hospital," I tell him. "I want to stay here, in my house, with my family."

"We can make that happen," he assures me. "But we also want to make sure you're comfortable."

I close my eyes and tug the covers up higher around me. I can feel the fatigue beginning to creep into my mind, his voice sounding farther and farther away, his words swimming through the fog, trying to reach me. I close my eyes—for just a minute, I promise myself. Just for a minute...

"I'm sorry," I say. "I'm just so tired. I can't stay awake anymore."

"It takes a lot of energy to do what you're doing," he says.

"But I'm not doing anything," I protest. Because what am I doing? I'm wasting away, barely even existing. I'm not doing anything.

"You're living. It takes energy and guts to do that, especially in the face of this."

"Not very well, apparently," I say quietly. I glance down at my bedspread, trace the pattern with my finger.

My mom's in the kitchen downstairs. I can hear her moving around, hear the rattle of bottles in the fridge as the door closes, hear the slide of a drawer being opened and then the clink of silverware soon after. I'd bet anything she's preparing a lunch tray with some faint glimmer of hope that I'll eat even a few bites. I wish more than anything I could do that. I wish I could get better for her.

"Dr. Wilhems?" I take a deep breath. "I need to ask a favor."

"Anything."

I lift my eyes to meet his, keep them locked there, resolute.

"I need you to tell my mom I'm going to be okay."

He inhales sharply. When he speaks, there's regret in his voice. "Lila, I can't—"

"I need you to lie to her," I plead. *I need you to lie to me.* "Just… Tell her there won't be any pain. Tell her—tell her whatever you need to so this is all okay."

A moment too late, I realize what I've said, realize how helpless he must feel—to be a doctor and not be able to save me—and I bite my lip and watch him, waiting as he processes what I've asked of him. He has deep wrinkles at the corners of his eyes and gray stubble that contrasts against his dark skin. His eyes are filled with sympathy, not pity, and I wonder how many times he's done this before. Wonder if anyone has ever asked him for this gift.

"This is never okay," he says softly.

Tears prick at the corners of my eyes, but I blink them away. "But I will be," I tell him, and for the first time, I start to believe it might actually be true. "I've had a lot of time to think about it, and I'm going to be okay."

For a brief second, there's pain etched across his face, and for the first time, I see his age there, like time has finally caught up with him after chasing him all these years.

He clears his throat, blinks back the shadow in his eyes. "My big sister used to say that, too, when she was sick. You're a lot like her."

"What happened to her?" I don't know if I want to know. I feel like I need to know.

"It was the tail-end of the war, so medicine was still hard to come by. Hell, everything was hard to come by back then." He shakes his head. "I still remember it like it was yesterday. I was twelve, just come home from school. My parents were busy working, so our neighbor was watching out for her, but then it was just the two of us. She wanted me to read to her, so I did—one of my comic books, if I recall. *Captain America.* Yes, that's what it was… I'd saved up just enough money to buy it myself." A small, proud smile flits across his face. "Some things you never do forget. When I finally stopped reading, she was smiling. She reached for my hand and told me—she told me…" His voice trails off, and he sighs like he's tired.

See? Time catching up. Time always catches up. I wonder how much time I have left before it catches up to me.

"Not a single day goes by that I don't think about her," he says. "She's what made me want to be a doctor."

"I think I would have wanted to be a doctor," I admit to him. "Maybe. I don't know."

I wish I'd had time to figure it out.

Dr. Wilhems smiles. "You keep being brave," he says. He pats my hand and stands up. "I'm not done fighting for you, sweetheart. You can be sure of that. There are breakthroughs happening every day. Don't you give up on me now."

I force a smile as my mom comes back into the room, as she hands me the pudding cup, as they chat in the doorway. I'm too tired to make promises I don't know if I can keep.

Chapter Forty-Nine

"This isn't fair."

"No."

"It's not fair."

"I know."

"No, I'm saying—"

"I know." A pause. "Lord help us, I know…"

I don't care how old I am today. I just don't care.

Chapter Fifty

LILAC

I'm watching *The Joy of Painting* on TV while Mom and Dr. Wilhems talk quietly in the hall outside my bedroom. I don't know why—there's a thousand movies I want to see, a thousand books I want to read, and only so much time. But I think that's it—knowing I'll never see everything I want to see or read everything I want to read or do everything I want to do makes me appreciate the tranquil nature of Bob Ross even more. His voice is soothing when he speaks, the brushstrokes on canvas mesmerizing, and the thought of creating something out of nothing leaves me spellbound.

I am something and will soon become nothing. Here is nothing becoming something—something beautiful, meaningful, timeless. The art of becoming. Maybe that's all we are, wrapped in this cycle of transformation like these scenic paintings on a blank canvas—nothing to something to nothing to something ad infinitum, forever, amen.

I want to be cremated. I tell them this when they come back in the room. Scattered in the soil among the roots of a tree so I can become something again—a maple or an oak or a willow tree, arms strong and outstretched towards the sky. I can see them exchange glances out of the corner of my eye, but I lean back against the pillows, turn up the volume on the TV, and smile serenely. I'll be something beautiful, meaningful, timeless.

Happy little ashes.

Chapter Fifty-One

This is how we really begin.

It's early March—that time of year when the grass is brown and the stray leaves in the flower beds are brittle and the sunlight casts a false sense of security across the landscape for how cold it is outside. Soon, we'll be shopping for swimsuits and sunglasses, if we're lucky and spring comes early. But today the weatherman is calling for a foot or more of snow, and I'm looking out the window, eyes trained on the low, gray clouds, eager to put on my snowsuit and gloves so I can build a fort in the yard and imagine I'm part of an expedition to Antarctica.

"You shouldn't put that there," Allison says over my shoulder. I pull my gaze from the window and stare at the tree I've just drawn in thick brown crayon. Its limbs are spread across the paper, reaching well past the sky.

"Why not?"

"Cause you're not going to have any room for the house."

I don't tell her she's right, that I've drawn the tree too big and now there's not enough space to draw my house—or the house next door, whose Sold sign was taken down this morning, and now we're all eagerly awaiting the arrival of our new neighbors.

Well, some of us more than others.

"I'm not drawing a house anymore," I tell my sister. "It's going to be a great big forest full of fairies and mermaids and—"

"We just read *Peter Pan*," my mom explains from the kitchen where she's clearing the breakfast table.

My sister shrugs. "Fine, whatever," she says and runs upstairs, slamming the door to her room.

Exactly one hour later, a moving truck pulls up in front of the house next door. We hear the squeal of its brakes, then the booming voice and heavy accent of someone outside. I rush to the bay window and see a man standing next to a green sedan in the driveway, gesturing angrily at his bare wrist.

"Mom! Mom! Mo-om!"

"Shush, Lilac, I'm right behind you."

"Oh." I glance over my shoulder and see my mom at the kitchen table, a mug of hot coffee beside her and checkbook in hand. "The moving truck is here."

The house next door has been empty all week, but I can still imagine every room, every square inch of wallpaper, every indent in the carpet where the furniture used to be. That's what happens when you have a best friend who lives a couple hundred feet away—their house becomes an extension of your own and, by proxy, an extension of you.

I don't like what's happening, as much as I want to watch what's happening. I don't want to imagine someone else eating dinner in their kitchen or watching Saturday morning cartoons in their living room. The house is Kate's and only Kate's, even though someone else belongs there now.

There's a minivan parked in the street in front of our house, a plastic cargo carrier strapped to the roof. Cardboard boxes with writing on the sides cover the maps Kate and I drew on her driveway in chalk her last day here, when the weatherman started calling for a storm and we planned our adventures even knowing we would be down a best friend by the end of the hour. I lean forward and press my cheek against the glass, trying to see better. It feels cold to the touch, but I don't mind. That just means snow's coming, and with the snow comes my now-solo trip to Antarctica.

A boy my age is turning in circles in the driveway, his head bowed. It takes me a minute to realize he's trying to decipher our maps.

"Mom!"

"For the love of God, Lilac," my mother says directly over my shoulder.

I jump, then giggle and press my fingers against the glass. A man is shouting at the little boy and pointing at the bicycle that lies in the path of the movers. The boy hurries to pick it up and rides it in slow circles down the driveway and out into the street.

I strain to see further up the driveway. "Do you think they have a dog?"

"I don't know, but it looks like their girls are Allison's age," my mom says, watching two pretty teenagers wander out of the garage and over to the minivan where they begin unloading suitcases and backpacks and gathering pillows in their arms. "I wonder if they'll babysit."

I frown. I'm six years old. I don't need a babysitter.

"I don't need a babysitter," I say, but my mom ignores me, and we watch the activity in silence for a moment until she tugs on the strap of my overalls.

"Get your shoes on. We don't want to be late for Gretchen's birthday party."

I make a face but don't budge. "When are we gonna meet them?"

"When they've settled in a bit," my mom says, grabbing her purse and car keys from the counter.

"When do you think that'll be?"

She ignores me, tugs on my overalls again, and thrusts Gretchen's birthday present in my hands. I begrudgingly grab my sneakers and coat and follow her out through the garage, where my dad is busy working on an overturned snow blower. I toss my coat and the present on the floor and work on wriggling my feet into my shoes.

"Did you see?" I ask my dad.

My dad grunts, digging through his toolbox. "What's that, kiddo?"

"We have new neighbors!"

He looks up, his eyes flicking past the open garage door to the street where large men are carrying a heavy couch down the ramp of the moving truck.

"Those are the Emerys," he says.

My eyes grow wide. Even my mom seems surprised.

"You've met them?" she asks.

"Sure," my dad says with a shrug. "They introduced themselves when they pulled up. Told them I'd take care of their sidewalks for them if it snows so they can get settled—soon as I get this thing fixed."

My mom and I exchange glances. There's so much I want to know—where are they from, is the little boy going to be in my class, do they have a dog—but my mom is already halfway to the car and telling me to hurry up.

"Are you buckled in?" my mom asks when I climb into the backseat. I nod and stare out the window as we back down the driveway. Next door, the movers are carrying a large oak dresser up the sidewalk, directed by a well-dressed woman standing in the open doorway and pointing up the stairs. The teenagers are digging through cardboard boxes in the garage, the little boy crouched beside them, like he's waiting for them to find whatever it is they're looking for. The man is nowhere to be seen.

I glance up at the gray clouds that still hover above us and gasp. Tiny white flakes are beginning to float down from the sky.

"Look, Mom! It's snowing!" I exclaim, but my voice is drowned out by the sound of metal crunching beneath our rear tire. The back of the car lifts, then falls again with a heavy thump as Mom slams on her brakes. Her eyes grow wide. She curses under her breath.

I roll down the window and poke my head out. Up at the house, the little boy has run halfway down the driveway, staring in horror at his broken bike beneath our car.

"Oh, my God," my mom says.

I stick my tongue out and catch a snowflake.

"At least it wasn't their dog," I say.

That's how I meet Nathan Emery.

Chapter Fifty-Two

I'm turning thirty-nine in a few days. And since I'm turning thirty-nine, which feels way too close to forty for comfort, I've decided it's time to reevaluate my life.

Steady job? It's status quo but pays the bills.

Travel the world? I got a postcard once from Paris, Tennessee.

Significant other? Dumped yesterday, thank you very much.

Okay, so maybe this is a bad idea. I don't like what I see, don't like what's happening here. Seriously, why can't I ever dream bigger for myself? I determine the best way to rectify this is to not think about the fact that I'm turning thirty-nine and instead go to the grocery store for ice cream. Lots and lots of ice cream.

Which is why I'm here at eight o'clock on a Friday night, leaning on a shopping cart as I roam the nearly-deserted aisles. Dramatic power ballads are belting from the store sound system. There are a handful of teens working the checkout lines at the front, and a single mother with a serene smile takes her time in the cereal aisle, having paid for a babysitter just so she can shop tonight in peace. There's a young couple ogling each other near the baked goods and a man in an expensive business suit in the freezer section packing a basket full of microwave dinners.

Then there's me.

"Lilac?"

I freeze. I don't want to see anyone I know tonight—especially not tonight, when I'm dressed in sweats and a ponytail and about to turn thirty-nine. Especially not when it's him. Of course it's him.

"Nathan?"

It's always him.

He breaks into a smile when I turn around, steps forward like he wants to come hug me, then realizes he has a package of instant coffee in his hand and puts it in his basket instead.

"Thought that was you. How have you been?"

"Good, fine," I say. "I've been fine."

Lost. Lonely. About to turn thirty-nine.

"You, uh…" He gestures vaguely to the boxes of coffees and teas lining the shelves. "You looking for anything in particular?"

"Nope." I reach out and grab the nearest box of tea. *Sleep Easy.* Sure, why not.

Nathan puts his basket down and steps forward, that smile still lighting up his eyes like he really is glad to see me. "What have you been up to? I haven't seen you in, what, ten years?"

It's more like twenty, but I guess time affects people differently when they've moved on.

"Twenty," he repeats. "Right. Not since graduation day. Well, what have you been doing with yourself? How are your parents?"

"Still together, still in the house on Peachtree," I tell him. At least I can always get that wish right. "How's your mom? I was sorry to hear about your dad."

"Yeah, well." He shrugs, but his jaw tightens. "I think we all saw that coming. At least Mom didn't have to watch him suffer in the end. If there's one good thing to come out of divorce, at least it's that."

"Yeah," I say. "At least there's that."

Our history crawls through the space between us, wrapping around us like this new, awkward silence. There's too much here—childhoods filled with birthday parties and summer barbecues and bus rides to and from school. There's not enough—twenty years of absence between then and now—and it feels like we're trying to make up for all that lost time in the space of a heartbeat in the middle of the hot beverage aisle of a too-bright grocery store.

"How have you been, Lilac?" He steps forward, and time squeezes us again. He still hunches slightly, like he never knows what to do with his height, and that one lock of hair still falls over his forehead. It disarms me, this sudden realization that some things never change, and I find myself wanting to inch my way towards him. "How are you really?"

"Oh, you know," I say. "Great job, great apartment, great life. I can't complain."

Oh, but I could... I really could, and you could watch me. We could be here hours before I even take a breath.

His smile widens. "That's great to hear."

I nod, glance away from him because I know what's coming. The words have been sinking to the bottom of my gut since the minute he said my name, and now they're ready to come to the surface and there's no avoiding them.

I don't want to hear their answer, but it's inevitable. I take a deep breath and expel them. "And you? How are you?"

"I'm doing great. The girls are ten and six now. I can hardly believe how fast everyone grows up—"

Well, some of us get that chance.

"We're building a house in Napa Valley."

I blink. "Wait, what?"

"Yeah. My architecture firm has taken off, so we bought some property in California for a vacation home. Up in the mountains with a view of the riverfront."

I stare at him. That's impossible. He's talking about my dream. That's been my dream since Kate sent me a postcard from her family trip in the second grade. I was awed by the blue of the water and the stretch of hills that seemed to cradle it. Only it's southern California, not northern. And that's the ocean, not the river. And besides, he's supposed to be an archeologist, not an architect. He's getting it wrong. He's getting it all wrong.

"Clean lines, picture windows, open floor plan…"

That should be me there, walking barefoot through an empty house. The white tile floor is cold to the touch but the sunlight warms the room through its floor-to-ceiling windows, a view of the bluffs to my right, the town to my left, and the expanse of ocean below. That should be Nathan there in the doorway, watching me inspect our design, this house we've built together. New appliances in the kitchen and a window ledge large enough for small potted herbs, grown fresh for cooking. A wall of hidden closets in the bedrooms, an old Hollywood vanity in the bathroom, and a window seat at the top of the stairs with three scenic views.

"Rachel wanted the window seat." He sounds so far

away, like the words belong to someone else, someone I never knew.

"Rachel?"

"My wife. She wanted a window seat for her reading, but I keep telling her the dog's going to claim it as his spot. Did I tell you we have a dog? A golden retriever named—"

"Lucky."

He cocks his head. "That's right. How'd you know?"

Because I always wanted a dog.

My feet sink into the new carpet as I wander the vacant house, soft to the touch like I'm floating on air, and that's how I feel now—like I'm floating away, distancing myself from this vision I'd created for myself, this fantasy he's spoiling with the mention of living it with someone else.

"This was my dream," I whisper, gazing out the windows at the view of soft sand beaches and pulsing waves. I don't like what's happening here. My own daydreams are becoming so tainted, there's no peace in them anymore.

He steps up behind me, kisses me on the cheek. "It should have been you," he whispers, but I shake my head.

I don't want to hear those words. They're too late, too late. This town, this house, this imagined life isn't mine anymore. Now, it belongs to him and his future wife and a dog named Lucky.

I can't do this. I can't hope and wish and dream anymore. I can't imagine the life I wish I had because it will never come true. I'll never be with him. This place will never exist. This lifetime I want will never happen.

I'm done dreaming. I don't have any left.

Besides, when you're too busy dreaming, there's no time left for living.

Chapter Fifty-Three

LILAC

Allison's on the phone. I can tell it's her because my mom keeps glancing over at me as she paces back and forth in the kitchen entryway while using words like "backsplash" and "fiberglass" and "laminate." I want to tell my mom she can sit down and have an actual conversation with her firstborn—that she doesn't have to keep checking on me—but it's one of the rare times I've felt strong enough to come downstairs in a week, and I can tell she's worried that might change any second now.

I'm not getting better. That's a fact. In fact, I'm slowly and steadily getting worse.

But more and more, I want to go for drives past my school, past the park, past the church where I used to go to Sunday school and attend holiday bazaars with my parents. I want to stretch my legs, feel what it is to stand at the fridge and pour a simple glass of milk for Santa, remember what it's like to crawl beneath the Christmas tree and gaze up at the lights like they're the stars I know so well, peeking through the branches in the willow trees out back. I want to walk from room to room, memorizing this house that's been my only home—every scratch in the floorboards, every picture on the mantle, every memory folded into the fabric of these walls.

That's why I'm here in the living room tonight, pretending to watch some sketch comedy on TV, half-listening to my mom talk to Allison about the latest episode in their bathroom renovation drama. I might be curled up on the couch, wrapped in my familiar hand-knit afghan, but I'm walking through my memories.

There on the brick hearth is where Nathan and I sat stringing popcorn for the Christmas tree when we were eight. We kept sneaking pieces for ourselves, and by the time we were finished, there was only enough popcorn left to trim half the tree. We have an artificial tree set up in the corner now. It's a little too early for Christmas, but Dad brought it over a few days ago, anyway, then spent half an hour in the basement looking for our ornaments. The box is opened and sitting in front of the fireplace, and from my place on the couch, I can see the homemade wreath I made out of dried apples when I was in kindergarten. Mom never throws anything away.

Hidden in the cupboard beneath the bookshelf are a handful of board games we used to play on Friday nights: *Sorry. Risk. The Game of Life.* We'd gather around the coffee table, slices of pizza on paper plates beside us, and spend the night listening to my mom's old *Beatles* records as we battled for Board Game Champion. When Allison started dating, Nathan took her place, but then as the years passed, my dad began working longer hours and my mom chose Friday nights to do her grocery shopping. It didn't matter at that point, anyway. I was too old for board games. And besides, Nathan was no longer welcomed here.

I look away from the cabinet. I don't feel like walking past those memories tonight.

Instead, I turn a different corner.

There, next to Dad's old recliner, is the side table with the faded stain from when I set my ice pop down and then promptly forgot about it. In the bay window, now outlined with Christmas lights, is where I used to read, piling it up with pillows so I could pretend it was a window seat. And there above the fireplace, nestled between pictures of me and Allison as kids, is my mother's Hummel collection—porcelain figurines from Germany that always reminded me of the fairytales she used to read me. Occasionally, I'd sneak them down from their spots on the mantle when my mother wasn't home, cradling them in my shirt and running upstairs to play with them in my dollhouse. I broke one when Allison was babysitting once. Chipped the hand right off when it fell off the roof. Allison helped me glue it back together so neither of us would get in trouble. I think that's the last nice thing she ever really did for me.

"Here." I glance up to see Mom holding out the phone. "Allison wants to talk to you."

"Why? Is she having trouble picking out her towel warmer?"

"Just get on the phone, Lilac!" I hear Allison yell.

My mom lifts an eyebrow, and I sigh and take the phone from her and watch her walk away. "Yes, oh, beloved sister," I say into the phone.

Allison sighs. "Why do you always have to be so difficult?"

"Because it's fun."

"Well, could you knock it off for five minutes?" She pauses. "I'm coming to see you next week. Kurt's finishing up the caulking in the bathroom, and I have some vacation time, so…"

"Did he get the bidet?"

"The what?"

"The bidet," I repeat myself. "I really want to know. I mean, Mom said you had to forego the Jacuzzi, so you might as well go all-in on the bidet."

"You're such a brat sometimes, you know that?"

I do, in fact, know that.

I glance at the clock on the mantle to see how long we've been talking. One minute and twenty seconds. Well, that's longer than any conversation we've had in almost a year, so kudos to her.

"Lilac?" my sister says. "Are you still—"

"Why?"

There's a long pause on the other end of the line. I can hear the TV on in the background, can almost make out what it is they're watching if she'll just give me a few more—

"Why what?" she asks, but I can tell she knows where I'm heading with this.

"Why are you coming to see me? I know you have stuff going on there. You don't have to come. I mean, unless you're coming because of Mom. You don't have to come because of me."

I want her to come because of me. I wanted her to come a month ago, three months ago, six months ago. But I haven't seen her in almost a year—since just a few weeks after her wedding, a few days before my birthday, when she and Kurt moved to Phoenix. She didn't ask to speak to me when I got out of the hospital the last time. She didn't call me when she found out I wasn't going back to school, and why. She didn't come to visit when Dr. Wilhems told us we had options, but not the kind of options we were hoping for. So why now? Why, when she thinks it matters most now, when it could have mattered more then?

"Mom called me a few days ago. She said it was time to come visit."

I blink. "Time to come visit? Jesus, it's not like I'm dying or anything. Oh, wait."

"Do you always have to be so morbid?"

"Do you?"

I'm trying to hide my anger, to forgive this resentment I have towards her, towards everyone, but I can feel it resurfacing. *I'm dying!* I want to scream at her. *I'm dying, and why the hell don't you give a damn?*

In who-knows-how-long she's not going to have a sister anymore and I—I'm going to melt into oblivion, and then where will she be? Wishing she'd been here sooner? It's too late for that. Who is she to come here now when I needed her then? When my mother was alone because Dad couldn't deal and Allison couldn't deal and Nathan couldn't deal, so it was just me and Mom. My sister doesn't deserve this. She doesn't deserve to be here now so she can feel good about herself and mourn me whenever the time comes. Fuck them. Fuck them for abandoning us.

"You used to idolize me, you know," Allison says quietly. If I didn't know any better, I'd swear there were shades of regret in her voice.

"I never idolized you."

"You did, though. You used to chase after me with your little bare feet and chubby cheeks and ask me to hold tea parties with you."

"Well, now I know you're lying because I definitely didn't do that."

"Grandma's tea set—the miniature one with the purple roses. Remember that?"

I fall silent. I do remember that, actually. Grandma used to keep it in the china closet in her living room. We were never allowed to go in there without her permission, and never with our shoes on. I remember the tea set. I used to love that tea set. I don't remember Allison.

"I'm trying my best," she says now.

Well, you're doing a shit job of it, I want to tell her. But I stay silent. It's this silence that enrages her.

"I can't believe you." I open my mouth, ready to fire back, but Allison's barreling through. "If you only knew, Lilac. Seriously, if you only knew." She sounds like she's on the verge of tears, and I glance down at my hands, wondering if I need to say something to make this better. Wondering why it's always up to me. "Look, I'm sorry I haven't been able to come out there sooner," she says. "But I'm coming now, alright?"

I stare at my lap, pull at a loose thread in the afghan so it begins to unravel. I hastily tuck it back into the folds. "I'm just saying, you don't have to," I mutter.

"Of course I have to, you're my little sister."

The tears surprise me. I didn't expect them. But now they burn my eyes and threaten to spill because I didn't expect her to say that, either. Her words make my heart expand, and I draw in a deep breath. This is my sister. My sister who always wanted me on her team for Game Night and who let me put the star on the Christmas tree and who helped mend one of Mom's broken figurines. My sister who I really did used to idolize, who hadn't abandoned me completely, who did want to see me—

"Besides, Jasmine just had her baby, so it's a good time to visit."

I stop breathing for a minute. Right there, on the couch in my living room, I forget to breathe.

"Lilac?" she asks. "Lila?"

But I've already hung up.

Chapter Fifty-Four

"I'm so sorry!" Allison wails, draping herself over my prone body. "I'm so sorry I didn't come to see you sooner. I'm so sorry I didn't care."

Extravagant bouquets of flowers grace windowsills and tables, and family and friends gather around my bed, dabbing at their eyes with sodden tissues. There are pictures of me along the walls, a collage of my life—smiling, happy, healthy. Neighbors are shaking their heads as they gaze upon them, sharing memories and stories and wondering how a life so full of promise could be taken too soon, too soon...

"Please forgive me, Lila," Allison cries. "Will you ever forgive me? Please forgive me..."

I'm not anything today. I'm not eleven or fourteen or sixty-six. I'm absent of age, like I'm absent of breath. I'm the sum of all my years and the division of all I had left, one cancelling out the other so that nothing remains—not anger, not fear, not forgiveness.

There's a zero within me.

Chapter Fifty-Five

LILAC

My mom picks up the phone from the other end of the couch where I've thrown it and places it on the coffee table. She pats my legs, and I struggle to lift them so she can sit down beside me.

"I don't want to talk about it," I tell her, draping my legs across her lap.

"You can't be mad at them forever, sweetie."

"I bet you I can."

I leave out the part we never talk about, about forever being only a few more months, weeks, days—however long I have left. But I think she realizes her choice of words because she blinks back tears, pats my legs again, and clicks off the TV. If it were anyone else—my sister or Dad or Nathan—I probably would have reminded them that forever has an expiration date, but not her. I'd never do that to her.

"She only wants to visit so she can see Jasmine's baby," I tell her. "She doesn't want to see me or be there for you. What kind of person does that? Who does that, who just ignores what's happening like that?"

My dad, that's who. And Nathan, who I haven't seen since the night of the wedding, the night the cold rain fell and the fever came. The night he took one look at the medicines on my dresser and me wrapped up in bed and bolted.

My mom was the one to tell me he moved out of his house the next day—presented an ultimatum to his mother and then packed a duffel bag and took off in his truck, but I didn't know where or how long he'd be gone. Apparently, his move was permanent. He might know what forever feels like, too.

"She calls almost every day," my mom says gently.

I glance at her, forgetting for a second who we're talking about. "Yeah, to talk about fucking faucets."

"Lilac—"

"It's such bullshit, Mom." My face is flushing with anger. I'm using energy I don't have, but I don't care. "She should be here and helping you because you shouldn't have to do this alone. You shouldn't have—"

"Lilac, your sister is helping me."

I pause and stare at her. "What do you mean?"

My mother sighs, rubs a hand across her forehead. "We didn't want you to know, but your sister's been helping me out financially. It's why they went to Tennessee for their honeymoon instead of the Bahamas. It's why Kurt's doing the renovations on the house himself."

I stare at her, trying to let all of this sink in. Allison's words suddenly make sense, and now they scream their echo in my mind: *If you only knew, Lilac. Seriously, if you only knew.*

"So that's why they're not getting the Jacuzzi?" I ask because I don't know what else to say. This doesn't make any sense. My mom forces a smile and rubs my leg.

"She took a second job to help pay for your home nurse. It's okay, it's okay," she says when she sees my eyes begin to brim with tears. She leans over to tuck my hair behind my ear. "We're all doing okay. Your dad turned down an offer with another company so he could keep your insurance. Now your hospital stays and medicine are covered, and we have some money in savings to help us get by. This isn't your burden, sweetheart."

But it is. It is my burden because I'm the one who's sick, and now everyone else has to pay.

"But it didn't help," I say quietly. A tear slips down my cheek. I don't bother wiping it away. "All of the hospital visits and medicines and supplements and the nurse, and it didn't help."

I don't say the words, but my mom hears them anyway. *I'm still dying.*

"Oh, but we had to try, Lilac," my mom whispers. Her eyes are red-rimmed, her voice shaking. I lean forward. She wraps her arms around me. "We had to try, darling girl. We would go to the end of the world for you. All of us."

I didn't know, I didn't know. I'd spent so much time hating them all that I didn't know.

And now it feels like it's all too late.

WINTER

Chapter Fifty-Six

LILAC

"Lilac?"

The voice is so soft, I think I imagine it, and I heave a sigh and pull the covers tighter around me.

"Sorry," I hear my mom say. "She's... Lilac? Can you wake up, sweetie? Your dad is here."

I open my eyes, blink until my mom and my dad come into focus.

"Hi," I say, trying to force a smile, but the word comes out croaked, and my smile turns into a coughing fit. I reach for the water-filled sports bottle I now keep tucked in a corner of my bed. My dad hesitates, like he wants to help, but instead folds himself into the chair beside me.

"I'll go make us some lunch."

My mom excuses herself, and I have half a mind to ask if I can come with her, if only to not be here with him. But she's gone before I can open my mouth, and I don't have the energy to be out of bed today, anyway. If I'll admit it to myself, there's a small part of me that wants to stay. His past visits have been too brief, few words passing between us. Maybe it's time and we owe this to each other.

"Where's your wife?" I ask my dad.

"Rebecca's at work. She'll come visit soon."

I don't tell him I don't have soon. It seems too harsh a reminder for both of us. So instead I say, "How was Bora Bora?"

"We went to Florida."

"Well, that was your second mistake."

My dad frowns and clears his throat and reaches into his pocket. "I, uh—I brought this back for you." He places the object in my hand. "I figured you could add it to your collection."

I stare at it, a lump rising in my throat. It's a nautilus shell made out of green Czech glass, so small it fits in the palm of my hand. I run my fingers along the spiraled grooves, hold it up in front of the window so it catches the light.

"It looks like the ocean," I say.

"Do you want me to..." He gestures to the windowsill, where the rest of my collection is lined up, but I shake my head no.

"I'll hold onto it for a while," I tell him. His lips turn up in a smile, showing the dimple in his left cheek that's usually hidden by his salt and pepper scruff. He's shaved since I last saw him, and now the dimple is on full display. "You look like Grandpa when you smile."

He tilts his head. "I do?"

I nod. I never noticed it before. I guess I never really took the time to. I never had to look at him to see him before because he was always just my dad, he was always there. Until the day I looked for him and he wasn't. Now there are lines creasing the corners of his eyes, and even his eyebrows boast wisps of gray. Time and his own abandonment has changed him from the father I knew to the stranger I see so that I recognize him, and I don't. I know him, and I don't. He's my dad and he's someone else, and I just want him to be my dad again. I swear I won't hate him anymore if he'll just be my dad again.

"Daddy…"

His breath catches at the word. He's silent, like he's not sure he's heard me right, but his chin quivers and his own eyes glisten. Maybe he never thought he'd hear me call him that again. Honestly, I didn't think I ever would. But the seasons are getting shorter and the sun's setting too quickly and there's no time—*there's no time*—and the flood of anger I've held onto for so long is washing away in the space of a second now that he's here.

"Daddy," I say again. The word is like a homecoming, splitting our hearts wide open, resentment pouring out like an old infection, ready to be cleansed and healed. "Daddy, are you going to stay?" I can't keep the plea from my voice, or the tears from sliding down my cheeks. "Please tell me you're going to stay."

He chokes back a sob, bows his head and kisses my hand. His shoulders are shaking, and I reach out and rest a hand on his balding head. He gathers me in his arms, and I cling to him and cry because this is all I've wanted. All this time, and him here and holding me like he used to when I was little is all I want because I'm tired and scared and I need my dad. I've always needed my dad.

"I'm going to stay, baby girl," he whispers, his own tears staining my shirt where they land. "I'm so sorry, I'm so sorry… My brave, beautiful girl. I swear I'll stay with you forever…"

For the first time in my life, forever doesn't feel long enough.

Chapter Fifty-Seven

I read a story once about a four-year-old boy with a terminal illness who packed a suitcase with his favorite toys and books and a pair of socks adorned with little red fire trucks. When his mom came into his room and saw it sitting on his bed, she asked him where he was going.

"I'm going home," he said with a wide smile.

She paused, confused. "But Sammy, love, you are home."

"No," the little boy insisted. "I'm going *home*."

I wish I could pack everything I love in a suitcase and take it with me, so I can carry a piece of this home into the next. I'd take the ocean-colored nautilus shell and my postcards from Kate with all of their thinking-of-you promises and maybe even the Hummel figurine with the crack in its hand—remains of the time Allison and I glued the broken pieces back together again. I'd take my favorite socks—gray with little purple stars that Rebecca bought for me in one of her care packages—and the afghan my mom used to tuck around me that now hangs off the back of the chair by my closet. Then, I'd add in the telescope and my star lamp and the piece of the plaster arm cast I saved from the summer before third grade, a sticker of a bird kept in perpetual flight and two words sharing its regret.

I'd wrap it all up in bubble wrap and tuck it into my suitcase and close the lid, and I'd be okay because I'd know that all these pieces of me, everything I've loved, were coming with me.

It's not what I really want. I don't want the cast or the figurine or the nautilus shell because that's not what really matters. Those are just things, and it's the people I want with me after all, in the end.

But I can't do that. That's not possible. And besides, I'm four years old today.

So my favorite socks it is.

Chapter Fifty-Eight

LILAC

I hear the doorbell ring—a faint, two-tiered song piercing through the dream. I want to get up, want to roll over and open my eyes and call downstairs asking who it is, but the sun is streaming through a break in the curtains and everything feels so warm and calm and light.

A deep male voice filters up the stairs, and through my haze I think it must be Dr. Wilhems again, or maybe my dad. They've both been coming to see me more frequently lately. Rebecca even brought some groceries over for my mom this morning, and then she and my dad both stayed for lunch. I listened to their conversation as best I could, smiling to myself when once or twice I heard them all laugh. I think, for a minute, that everything's okay, and that's all that matters now—that they'll be okay.

The front door closes, and I hear footsteps on the stairs. I turn my head to glance at the clock. It's half past three. There's a soft knock on my door.

"I'm awake," I croak and cough, trying to rid the sleep from my voice.

The door nudges open, and my breath catches. It's not who I'm expecting. I'm expecting anyone but him.

"Lilac Sophia." He hesitates in the doorway, but a hint of a smile plays at the corners of his mouth. I try to hide my own smile, but it's him, he's here, and not just in a dream.

"Took you long enough, Emery."

He's cut his hair since the last time I saw him. Now short strands stick up in the front. And he's filled out, too, though he still hunches slightly from his height.

"Can I…" He gestures to the chair beside my bed, and I nod and reach for the water bottle beside me, partly to ease the rawness in my throat, partly because I need a few seconds to process the fact that Nathan is here—that I'm not imagining this—and now I don't know what to say.

When I turn to look at him again, his eyes are still on me. I feel my heart flip because I didn't expect that, either. This isn't the Nathan I remember—the Nathan who kept his gaze focused on the floor because he couldn't bear to look at me the last time he was here. The Nathan who didn't know what to say or do, so he ran. The Nathan who hasn't come back since.

This isn't that Nathan. This Nathan is confident, assured, grown up. I wonder when, in the space of the year since we last saw each other, that happened and how.

"How did you find out?" I ask because we may as well get this over with now. There's no room here to be polite, no time in which to shield ourselves from what's meant to come. We're excavating our past, digging up all those broken pieces like we did when we were kids and hunting in the creek for dinosaur bones. I can't help but wonder what we'll uncover today. I can't help but wonder how deep we'll dig.

"I always knew," he says, and I can hear it—shades of the old Nathan, diffidence sneaking up behind the smirk. He clears his throat. "My mom—she's, uh, she's been keeping me updated."

"You're staying with your sister?"

He nods. "I moved out the day after the wedding. But I come over to check on her sometimes." He pauses. "I even came over to see you, after you got out of the hospital."

I raise my eyebrows and glance at the window.

"Yeah," he says, following my stare. "I called your name, but I guess you didn't hear me."

I heard him. I heard everything. There's a lump in my throat, and I take a moment, squeezing my eyes closed, before turning back to him.

"Once," I say to him. "You called my name once. Was the doorbell too much for you? Or how about the phone? I mean, you could've gone old-school and sent a courier pigeon, but, hell, that might've meant you actually cared."

He exhales slowly. "Come on, Lilac. What do you want me to say?"

I know what I want him to say. Maybe he even knows what I want him to say. But I'll never hear those words. So instead I'll settle for echoes of the past—two words in fading marker written below the sticker of a bird on a third-grade cast.

"Never mind," I say instead, turning away from him. There's nowhere to go. "It doesn't matter."

"Bullshit. It does matter. And don't tell me I don't care, Lilac, because—because…"

"Because what?" I challenge him.

He grits his teeth, runs a hand through his hair. "God, you drive me crazy sometimes, you know that?"

"Yeah, well, join the club."

"Why is it so difficult with you?"

"With me?" I scoff. "Are you kidding me? Where were you, Nathan?" Tears are brimming in my eyes, ready to spill out with each word I utter. I can't forgive him like I did Allison, like I did my dad. It's not so easy this time, not with him. "Where did you go?"

He ducks his head, runs a hand across the back of his neck, but I see it flicker in his eyes even as he tries to hide it. Regret. Maybe that's enough. It should be enough, to know that someone is sorry. It should be enough to know that he's here now. I don't know why it isn't, and I don't know what kind of person that makes me that I can't just let it be enough.

"It was too much." His voice is so low, I almost don't hear him. He lifts his head, his eyes locking on mine, begging me to understand. "It was too much, Lilac. That night with my dad… And then you were so sick, and I didn't know what to do."

"Awesome. So you were afraid. Well, so am I." I tug at the IV line to make my point, watch his eyes flick towards it, then dart away. "I'm scared every single day. But I don't get to run away from this."

"I wasn't running away from it."

"You were running away from me."

"No." His eyes flash angrily. "No, no way."

"Then what were you doing?"

"I was—I was—" He shakes his head, rises to his feet and crosses the room. "Fuck!" he shouts and slams the palm of his hand against the doorframe before turning back around to face me. "I wasn't running away from you, Lilac. I would never do that."

But he did do that. When we were eleven and surrounded by a galaxy of stars, he ran away because of me and now we all know how history repeats itself.

I don't know what to say to him. For the first time in my life, I don't have some witty remark. My head is buzzing with thoughts, my heart racing with feelings, and I don't know how to decipher any of it. I want to yell at him and tell him how much I hated him for abandoning me again—like Allison, like my dad. I want to cry that he was my best friend, my only friend, and how could he just leave like that, how could he run out on me when we were eleven—and again when I needed him most—and never come back?

"That wasn't because of you," he says quietly.

"What?"

"Back then on your birthday—I can tell it's what you're thinking. Lilac, believe me, it wasn't because of you."

We're eleven years old right now. I hate being eleven. I sigh and lean back against the pillows.

"It was because you liked Amanda Zeleski," I remind him. He doesn't say anything, and suddenly I'm standing there in my bedroom on my birthday again, surrounded by stars and entirely alone.

"I know that's what I said."

"It's what you meant." I shrug and stare down at my hands. "It's fine. It's fine, really it is. I mean, it sucked, but it's fine. It doesn't matter now, anyway."

We're not eleven anymore.

He leans against the door, stares at the floor and scuffs the carpet with his sneaker. I tie a loose thread from my comforter in a knot, then another, then one more. The silence lingers in the space between us—a melancholic void that's miles wide.

"Do you remember that night?"

I gape at him. He's got to be joking.

"Are you joking?"

"No—Look, I know I was an asshole." He steps closer. "But I mean before that, when I came over for dinner."

"You were always coming over for dinner. Nate, we were best friends…"

That was the whole point—that one minute he was my best friend and the next, he wasn't. One minute he was always there, and the next he was gone, and though that was the first time, it wasn't the last. What wasn't he getting?

"Yeah, but I had my backpack with me that night, remember?" There's a plea in his eyes, like he's begging me to understand where he's going with this. But I don't understand. "Your mom came to the door and asked me if we had homework, and I told her yes. And then we had dinner and went outside to look at the Pleiades, and I gave you your birthday present."

I glance at the lamp that's still on my nightstand. It's buried behind a pile of books and supplement bottles, but I can still see a few darkened stars peeking out. Nathan follows my gaze and inhales sharply. He walks over to it, raises his hand like he wants to touch it, then shoves his hands in his pockets and stares out the window instead.

"There was more than that in my bag," he says quietly. "That was the night my dad took a swing at me." I stare at him, unable to speak. "He fell. Mom screamed. I ran upstairs and packed my bag and swore I'd never step foot in that house again. Then I came here. It was the only place I could think of, the only place I wanted to be, the only place I felt, I don't know, *normal*." He takes a deep breath and raises his eyes to meet mine. "I wasn't running away from you, Lilac. I swear, I'd never do that."

He was running to me. To us. To his best friend and my parents who were like his family because his own family was falling apart. He'd needed us, and I'd messed that up. Here was his only place of safety, of refuge, and I'd taken that away from him. I'd destroyed our friendship with one stupid kiss. In the end, I had abandoned him.

And now I know the words are mine to offer.

"I'm so sorry, Nate."

"Don't—don't." He sits on the edge of my bed, and he's so close, I want to touch him, to hug him. I want him to always stay this close. "You couldn't have known—I didn't want you to know. But after that…"

After that, everything changed.

"I don't know what happened to us, Lilac," he says. "I wanted to come back so many times, but I just couldn't. For a while, I was afraid to leave my mom alone with him. And by then, you weren't speaking to me, either."

"I spoke to you."

"Barely."

"When I had to," I concede, my lips drawn in a frown. "I think Allison's wedding was the first meaningful conversation we'd had in years."

His eyes light up. "For a while there, it felt like we were back on track, didn't it?"

"I told you I hated you."

"You tell me that all the time, and you never mean it."

"I really do." But I smile. I really don't.

Nathan shakes his head. "I hated that you had to see that with my dad. I felt—I don't know what I felt, but I didn't want you to see that. And then you were sick and I saw all the medical stuff and your mom came in yelling at me, and it made it all real, you know? All of it. This—" He takes a deep breath and looks around the room. "Jesus, this is real."

I know. Believe me, I know.

"I didn't know how bad it was for you until that night," he continues, his voice barely above a whisper. "I didn't know."

"Isn't that the point?" I ask softly. "Does anyone ever?"

He hears the refrain in those words, spoken nearly a year ago on a rain-soaked winter night. His mouth turns upwards in a sad smile.

I want to be mad at him. I want to yell at him and cry and hate him because it would make this so much easier. But most of all, I want to forgive him because he's here now, staring at me with pleading eyes, and I still love him. I still love Nathan Emery. And if there's one thing I know for certain in this whole fucked-up world, it's that I'll never stop.

His fingers brush my hand, and I forget to breathe. I stare down at the way his hand folds over mine, his thumb running back and forth across my skin. For a second, I wonder if I'm imagining this moment like I've imagined a thousand others before it. But it feels real. He feels real. I can't explain how much I need this to be real.

We sit in this silence together—him, gazing out the window, and me, studying him. I remember the way his hair used to dip past his eyes, how I always wanted to reach up and brush it away. His hair is shorter now—he's a different Nathan on the surface—but that boy is still there underneath. That boy who was my neighbor, my best friend. The boy I fell in love with. I want to remember every moment with him as he was, memorize every inch of him as he is here because I need this memory to last now, now that I'm the one that's leaving.

I break the silence.

"Nathan?"

"Yeah?"

"Will you promise me you'll get a dog?"

He looks surprised, like he expected anything but that. "A dog? You want me to get a dog?"

I nod. "Someday. And I want you to name him Lucky."

"You want me to get a dog and name him Lucky," he repeats.

"Yep."

He glances out the window, runs a hand across the back of his neck and exhales deeply. "I—Okay. I mean, I always wanted a golden retriever."

I smile. "I know."

"You're something else, Lilac Sophia."

I know that, too.

"Hey, Nathan?"

"You're not gonna ask me to adopt a sea turtle or anything now, are you?"

I laugh. "No. Not a sea turtle." I glance down at our hands, at the way they remain interlocked in this permanent bond of him and me. "I just want you to know I've missed you."

These moments are going by so quickly now. I don't know how many are left.

Chapter Fifty-Nine

NATHAN

Fuck.

I really don't want to do this. I can't even begin to explain how much I don't want to do this. Seeing Lilac like that was hard enough, why do I have to double down on this today? Yet here I am, standing outside this door that I should be calling home as the sun begins to set, wondering what's on the other side and if anything has changed at all.

It was something she said. Lilac, that is. Something about her dad. Something about forgiveness that I can't seem to shake. I shake my head. I should just leave well enough alone—come back another day, a different decade. He hasn't changed. There are still empty liquor bottles in the recycling bin that prove he hasn't changed. So why should I care? Why should I be here? Why should I be the one stepping up and acting like a father when the father is the child. This is such bullshit!

I kick at the front step and whirl around, throwing my hands through my hair in frustration as I make it a few steps down the sidewalk towards my truck. It's Lilac that stops me. It's knowing that she's there, a hundred yards away in her room, that prevents me from pulling my keys out of my pocket, getting in that truck, and never looking back. Because if Lilac could forgive me, then maybe…

I sigh and trudge back up the porch steps.

Ring the doorbell. That's all I gotta do. Hug Mom. Look him square in the eyes and say everything I need to say.

Say nothing.

Let the silence say everything.

I take a deep breath. I ring the doorbell. This isn't my house anymore. Not my home. Strange thing is, that thought no longer feels like a sucker punch to the gut, and maybe that's something. Because maybe my dad hasn't changed for shit—and that's okay because I don't expect anything else—but I have. I've changed. Maybe that's what makes the difference.

I almost step back when the front door flings open seconds later because there he is, looking just as shocked to see me as I am to see him. He's clean shaven. That's the first time I've seen him without a full beard since I was a kid. He's wearing a light blue work shirt, and though the sleeves aren't rolled up, there's a tie draped across his shoulder, like he just took it off. It's his eyes, though—clear and focused. And there's not a whiff of alcohol anywhere on him.

Huh. Sure as hell didn't see that coming.

I shift from foot to foot. The whole plan has changed now. Maybe everything's changed.

I say the only thing that comes to mind.

"Hi, Dad."

Chapter Sixty

"Goodnight, sweetie."

"Night, Mom… Wait, Mom?"

"Do you need something?"

"No, it's just—was Nathan here today?"

"You don't remember?"

"Maybe… I don't know."

"Should I call—"

"No, I'm fine. I just…Was he here?"

"He was here. Could barely get him to leave. He said he'll be back tomorrow, so you just get some rest."

"Tomorrow…"

"Are you sure you're okay?"

"I just wanted to be sure, that's all."

"Okay then. Sweet dreams, baby girl."

"Sweet dreams, Mom."

Sweet dreams.

Chapter Sixty-One

LILAC

Next week is my birthday. I should be turning seventeen and in my junior year of high school. I should be prepping for the SATs and thinking about colleges. I should be choosing my dress for the junior prom.

But I'm sixteen years old today.

I'll be sixteen years old for the rest of my life.

Chapter Sixty-Two

Sometimes I wonder how wildly altered my life would have been if even just one piece of it was different. Not the course of it—nothing could change the fact that I had an incurable illness, I know that. And maybe it couldn't even change my parents' divorce or Allison living out in Phoenix or Kate moving away. But if Nathan hadn't moved in next door when I was six, if we hadn't spent the year looking through my telescope when I was ten, if he hadn't driven me to my sister's wedding when I was about to turn sixteen, would I have been the same?

Maybe. Maybe not. Maybe I wouldn't have cared about the stars so much. Maybe I wouldn't have dared to dream about the life I could have lived. Maybe I wouldn't have tried to hold on to all of this so tightly.

But that's the thing about loving Nathan Emery. Somehow, every road always led me back to him. And I wouldn't have imagined it any differently.

"Are you sure you wanna be out here?" He shoves his hands in the pockets of his coat and burrows the tip of his nose in the zipped-up collar.

We're walking down my street, darkened by the hour

but glowing beneath the moonlight so the snow that blankets the landscape seems to glisten with an endless sheen. We've finally had a cold snap—icicles cling to tree limbs like teardrop chandeliers and stray snowflakes drape across lilac bushes in the gardens that line the road. The houses give way to clusters of trees as we walk, a forest growing dense around us.

"Lilac, maybe we should go back."

A light breeze pushes through and stirs the leaves still on the trees, making the icicle chandeliers chime a wistful melody in tune with the finches that flit among their canopy. I tilt my head back, close my eyes, and exhale. My breath swells in the air, gathering into a fog before climbing higher and higher and vanishing completely.

"Soon," I promise. "I just want to feel the wind."

Oh, but it's so much more than that. I want to walk down this road that's both familiar and strange. I want to nestle my bare feet in the fresh-fallen snow and feel the faint tickle of cold on my arms. I want to turn my eyes to the sky.

The stars have never looked like this before—alive with their own pulse and so close, I feel like I'm dancing among them. I giggle and step into the middle of the road, spread my arms and twirl, my dress billowing behind me in a flourish of pale purple. The stars are above me, below me, surrounding me. I'm swirling in a sea of constellations, dancing across galaxies.

"Lilac..."

He's calling to me, and I slow my dance at the plea in his voice, am struck still by the grief in his eyes. It's the two of us again, alone on a moonlit street in the middle of winter.

The trees are bare of their leaves. The icicles are cold and stoic. The stars are back where they belong.

"I like the way you say my name," I say softly and step closer. "It sounds like springtime."

He draws a shaky breath, clenches his jaw and looks away.

"Nathan—"

"Jesus, Lilac," he breathes and folds his arms around me, crushing me against him. He buries his face in the crook of my neck, tangles his fingers in my hair. "You're my best friend. What am I gonna do without you now? What the hell am I supposed to do?"

I wrap my arms around his neck, rest my chin against his shoulder.

"*Everything*," I whisper.

We hold each other for eternity. We hold each other for a minute. I'm the first to pull away. Nathan hesitates, squeezes my hand tighter like he's afraid to let it go.

"I love you," he says, and my lips spread into a smile.

"I've waited forever to hear you say that. And look—" I spread my arms. "Here we are."

"Don't joke." There are tears in his eyes, and he swallows and pulls me tight against him again. "Please don't joke."

I reach up and cup his cheek in my free hand. "Promise me you'll think of me? Cause I swear, Nathan Emery—I'll always be thinking of you."

Maybe that's all people want when the end comes around—and it always comes around. Maybe they just want to know that you'll be thinking of them—remembering every precious moment—and that you changed their life as much as they changed yours. Because if there's one thing

I know, it's that life may have kept me sick, but knowing Nathan made me better.

I feel something damp land on the back of my hand, and for a second, I think he might be crying. But we both look up. Flower petals float like snowflakes around us—shades of purple brushing past on the breeze. The trees are growing dense around us again, icicle chandeliers swaying in the breeze and singing a prayerful tune.

Nathan reaches for my hand. "Come on, let's go back inside," he pleads, but I slip out of his grasp.

"Can't. Gotta go." I smile and turn away. "See ya sometime, Emery."

These woods are lovely, dark, and deep…

And so I sleep, and so I sleep…

ALSO FROM THIS AUTHOR

GOLD IN THE DAYS OF SUMMER
(A NOVELLA)

2015 International Book Awards' Children's Fiction
Category Finalist

*"Pogorzelski captures the sense of a girl holding onto the
last days of a waning childhood."*
– Publisher's Weekly

*"An excellent, well-written and atmospheric story that
looks at growing up, family life, love and understanding."*
– International Rubery Book Award,
Children's Category Winner

THE LAST LETTER

2018 Writer's Digest Self-Published Book Awards
Honorable Mention

*"Pogorzelski's exceptional debut shares the challenges,
dreams, fleeting optimism, and difficulties of 15-year-old
Amelia Lenelli at the turn of the millennium."*
– Publisher's Weekly

*"The themes of loneliness and connection, despair and
perseverance, and beauty in the midst of ugliness are timeless
and vital to teen readers looking for something positive in
life and in the world around them."*
– 25th Annual Writer's Digest Self-Published Book
Awards

COMING SOON

ASHES IN AUTUMN (A NOVELLA)

EAST OF EVERYWHERE

Visit the author's website at
www.susanpogorzelski.com
to learn about upcoming books!

www.ingramcontent.com/pod-product-compliance
Lightning Source LLC
Chambersburg PA
CBHW021006120726
47905CB00009B/2881